YOU OWE ME ONE, UNIVERSE

AMULET BOOKS • NEW YORK

YOU OWE ME ONE, UNIVERSE

CHAD LUCAS

Cataloging-in-Publication Data has been applied for and may be obtained from the Library of Congress.

ISBN 978-1-4197-6686-2

Text © 2023 Chad Lucas
Illustrations © 2023 Nick Blanchard
Book design by Marcie Lawrence and Chelsea Hunter

Printed and bound in U.S.A.
10 9 8 7 6 5 4 3 2 1

Amulet Books are available at special discounts when purchased in quantity for premiums and promotions as well as fundraising or educational use. Special editions can also be created to specification. For details, contact specialsales@abramsbooks.com or the address below.

Amulet Books® is a registered trademark of Harry N. Abrams, Inc.

ABRAMS The Art of Books
195 Broadway, New York, NY 10007
abramsbooks.com

For the people who build refuges—in libraries and gyms,
workshops and music rooms—where kids can come alive

1. LIFE PART II

BRIAN

I wouldn't do well in jail. Just visiting stressed me out.

Everything about the place—beige concrete, tiny windows, guards in heavy vests—screamed *you're stuck here*. I knew that was the point, but feeling stuck was one of a dozen things that set off my anxiety hyperdrive. The second time I visited my dad here, I got dizzy, started sweating buckets, and nearly barfed. A correctional officer had to call a nurse, and it turned into this whole embarrassing scene.

I hated embarrassing scenes almost as much as I hated panic attacks, so put them together and it was Brian Day's perfect nightmare. But I still showed up most Sunday afternoons, because it was the only way to see my dad.

I made it through the first steps OK this time: checked in, got through the scanner to make sure I wasn't smuggling anything, followed an officer to the visiting room where Dad and I would have an hour together. My breathing was shallow and my face tingled, but that was only average nerves and not full panic.

Waiting was the hardest part. My brain went to weird places until Dad showed.

Worst-Case Scenarios: Jail Edition
1. *The jail will go into lockdown, and I won't get to see Dad.*
2. *Someone jumped him and he's bleeding out while I sit here waiting.*
3. *The guards have been possessed by murderous alien spores, and I'll have to use my wits to rescue Dad and stage a daring escape.*

My therapist, Dr. Bender, told me it was OK that I couldn't always stop my worst thoughts. Most people couldn't. But she said when I started going bleak, I should picture the most absurd worst-case scenario I could imagine. Sometimes this worked. In my mind, I was crawling through air ducts like I was in *Die Hard* when the door opened and Dad stepped in.

He crossed the room and pulled me into a hug. He never used to be a hugger, but now he squeezed me like he was trying to imprint me into his chest. I hugged him back just as hard.

Eventually he let go and held me at arm's length. "Sheesh, B-Man. You grow another inch this week? You'll be ducking through doorways soon."

He was exaggerating, but I'd grown four inches in five months since I turned thirteen. I had to buy all new pants for school.

Dad's eyes drifted toward the door. "Your mom's not here?"

I swallowed. "Uh, no. She was going to come, but Richie, uh . . ."

"I get it." Dad forced a smile. "Can't blame him. I'd rather not be here either."

If he was upset that my ten-year-old brother refused to visit, *again*, he hid it well. We sat. My eyes drifted to the officers by the doors and the other families huddled at tables with their loved ones. I'd been coming for four months, and I still wasn't used to this setup, all these people and emotions in one room with hardly any privacy. That's another thing you didn't really get in jail.

"So, how's school?" Dad prompted, and I tried to tune everyone else out.

"Ezra and I got a perfect grade on our presentation in social studies," I told him. "Ms. Virth loved it. Ezra did most of the talking, but I read two paragraphs out loud and didn't faint."

He grinned. "Congratulations, B-Man. I'm proud of you."

That was a big achievement for me. I still struggled with Super Awkward Weirdo Syndrome—that's what I called social anxiety. (Dr. Bender liked my nickname so much, she told me she shared it with other kids.) But I'd made some friends over the summer and I wasn't as terrified as I was when I started junior high last year.

The hour passed too quickly, and before I knew it, Dad was hugging me again. This time he held on longer, like he was stretching out every second he could. When he finally let go, he immediately turned toward his exit.

He never looked back. I don't think he liked me seeing how sad he was when our time was up. I still knew. But I got it. I didn't like watching him head back to his cell alone either.

The pre-visit anxiety was hard enough, but the ache in my chest when I left was worse. We were studying percentages in math, and I figured out that an hour was 0.595 percent of a week. That's how much of my time I got to spend with Dad. Less than one percent.

He was serving a twelve-month sentence, so this was our life until next July. I knew one year was a small percentage of the average person's life, but right now, it felt like forever.

Some people might say he deserved it. He did help run an illegal cannabis operation, even though he never hurt anyone and cannabis would be legal in Canada this time next year. But I didn't know who it was helping to keep him locked up. Certainly not us.

I shivered and zipped up my coat as I stepped back into the cold November air. We were into the bleak part of fall, when the leaves had fallen and winter was just around the corner.

Gabe was waiting for me, and I climbed in the back seat of his car, next to Ezra.

"How'd it go?" Gabe asked.

"Fine. The usual."

"Want to talk about it?" Brittany asked from the passenger seat.

"Not really."

They didn't push. Ezra handed me a paper cup. "Hope you're cool with hot chocolate. Brittany wouldn't let me buy you anything with coffee."

Brittany glanced back. "I'm still not over the time I made you a latte and you started yelling about parallel realities. I can't handle caffeinated Brian."

"No one can handle caffeinated Brian," Gabe said. "The world's not ready."

Ezra laughed. Ezra had curly black hair and stylish glasses and the best laugh in the world.

As Gabe drove, he and Brittany haggled over music. Ezra teamed up with Brittany for the win, as usual. By the time we reached the Mackay Bridge headed back to Halifax, they were singing along to some indie band they both loved. Gabe pretended he was annoyed, but it was impossible not to enjoy Ezra and Brittany singing. Ezra took the melody and Brittany sang harmony and they sounded amazing.

Gabe and Brittany were high school seniors, while Ezra was in the eighth grade with me. These three really kept me afloat when the universe collapsed a few months ago and Dad went to jail. They still kept me afloat now.

Gabe and Brittany dropped us off at Ezra's house. I tried to stifle my yawns while Ezra fixed us a snack, but he noticed.

"You need a nap, don't you."

I yawned again. "Sorry I'm so pathetic."

He tossed an Oreo at me. "No biggie. Go ahead."

I couldn't help it. Visiting Dad wore me out, even though I was glad I did it. I headed to the basement and flopped onto Ezra's bed. The Ezra-ness of his room was always comforting: band posters on the wall, guitars on a stand in the corner, the smell of his coconut-scented hair gel on the pillow. I usually slept well here.

Except today I had a nightmare. Or a napmare, I guess.

Dad was trapped in a cell filling up with water. It was nearly to the ceiling and he was running out of air. I found Mom and begged her to help me, but she was asleep. I shook her and shook her but she wouldn't wake up.

I must have been yelling in my sleep. When I jolted awake, Ezra was at the edge of the bed. I sat up and buried my face in my hands, waiting for the echoes of my fear to fade. Ezra put a hand on my back.

"Did you know, in 2004, a Dave Matthews Band tour bus emptied its sewage tank off a bridge in Chicago, right as a boat was passing underneath?" he said. "A bunch of people got drenched in eight hundred pounds of pure nastiness."

I blinked. "What? Are you making that up?"

"No, it's true, I swear. You can look it up." Ezra squeezed my shoulder. "So, whenever you wake up from a

6

nightmare, you can take a deep breath and remind yourself, *At least I'm not covered in poo from Dave Matthews Band.*"

He said this completely straight-faced. Then his lip twitched, and we both lost it. When I stopped laughing, I felt like 87 percent better.

This was peak Ezra. He knew how to make me laugh and get me out of my own head. And for reasons I didn't totally understand, he also had a crush on me.

My feelings for him were more complicated. Most things were complicated with me. But I'd been thinking lately that I needed to figure out what I really felt, for Ezra's sake. He deserved that. He deserved the whole world.

"Mom said she'll pick up some takeout on her way home," he said. "You feel like pizza or fish and chips?"

"Fish and chips," I said, surprising him. Usually I went with *doesn't matter* or *you pick.*

He grinned. "Feeling decisive?"

"Trying."

He stood, and I untangled myself from his bedsheets. *Be more decisive* was a sub-goal on my multi-step plan for surviving Life Part II. And I wanted to start with my best friend.

2. BOHEMIAN RHAPSODY

EZRA

"Here's one," Kevan said, which meant he was about to throw out some wild idea. "Imagine everyone had to get a tattoo on their butt. What would yours say?"

Kevan and Ty showed up after Brian and I finished dinner. Now we were chilling in my basement, talking nonsense. And butt tattoos, apparently.

Kev sat cross-legged on the floor, and I poked him with my foot. "Why do we need butt tattoos?"

He swatted my foot away. "Some evil dictator is in charge and he's into mandatory butt tats."

"One cheek or both?" Brian asked.

"Doesn't matter. You're overthinking it."

"It matters," Brian insisted. "My butt's as skinny as the rest of me. I need to know what surface area I'm working with."

Ty snickered, and Brian broke into the grin he got whenever he made a successful joke. He was quiet in public,

8

but when the four of us were goofing around, he unleashed his inner comedic weirdo.

Ty scooped a handful of chips. "My butt tattoo would say *Chosen*."

Kevan took the bait. "Why *Chosen*?"

"If we're stuck in an evil butt-tattoo dictatorship, I'm the Chosen One who kicks their butts." Ty hopped up and wiggled his butt at Kevan. "My *boot-ay* saves the day."

"*Behold, the ancient prophecy is fulfilled,*" I declared in my deepest wizard voice as Kevan squirmed away from Ty. "*The season of the full moon has come. Tyrone shall deliver us by the power of his derriere.*"

Nineteen butt jokes, a wrestling match, and one earth-rumbling Ty fart later, we were weak with laughter. Brian sprawled out on his belly with his hands tucked under his chin and let out a contented sigh.

It made me happy to see him so happy, especially after visiting his dad and having a bad dream this afternoon. I tried not to worry about him too much. He didn't like making his friends worry.

I also tried not to think about how cute he looked right now, all stretched out on the floor.

It wasn't like I thought about that all the time. Maybe 36 percent of the time. OK, maybe more like 49 percent.

We debated what movie to watch for a while and finally settled on a comedy about two nerdy high-school best friends who decide to go wild on prom night. It was hilarious, but there was a scene near the end where a romantic song kicked in on the soundtrack and they realized they were in love with each other and then shared a passionate kiss on a balcony.

Kevan nodded in Brian's direction. "Now I see why you wanted to watch this movie," he whispered.

I poked him with my foot again. "It was Ty's pick."

I risked a glance at Brian. He was watching the screen intently and not saying anything.

Kevan and Ty went home after the movie, but Brian stayed. We had Monday off for Remembrance Day, and he was spending the night. He fell into his distant, brain-churning-at-warp-speed type of quiet once we were alone. Brian had at least six levels of quiet and I was learning to tell them apart.

"What do you want to do?" I asked. "Another movie? Arm-wrestle? Write a song?"

He didn't answer for a while. "Do you think it really works like that?" he finally asked. "Like in the movie? People can be friends for a while, and then they suddenly realize they want to be . . . more?"

His freckled cheeks flushed.

I gulped. "Uh, I don't think it's as dramatic as the movies. And the kissing probably isn't as messy."

Brian nodded. "They looked like they were trying to eat each other's faces."

"I think that was for comedic effect maybe. Not that I'm an expert on kissing or anything."

I cringed. *Why did I say that?* Talking about kissing was

making weird things happen in my head. And I might have been sweating behind my ears. That was definitely weird.

"Me neither. But, um." Brian scratched his neck. "I've been thinking. You know how you have feelings for me . . ."

Now my face was on fire. One advantage of having brown skin was it helped hide my embarrassment, but I was sure Brian could still tell.

"And I've been kind of . . . not sure," he continued.

I straightened my glasses. "Is this because of the movie? We don't have to talk about it."

"I know," he said quickly. "And it's not because of the movie. Well . . . I guess it made me think about stuff. But I was already thinking about stuff." His face was bright red now. "I'm not explaining this very well. Honestly, Ezra, I don't know how I feel. I like the *idea* of liking you. You're my favorite person in the world."

This made me feel a different kind of warm all over.

"But I overthink everything, right? So maybe I need to stop thinking. Maybe the best way to figure it out is . . ." He paused for an eternity. "We should try, you know. Kissing."

I blinked. *Did I hear him right?* One sentence ran on a loop in my mind, and I turned it over in every possible way.

Brian wants to kiss me?

Brian *wants* to kiss me?

Brian wants to *kiss* me?

Brian wants to kiss *me*?

Brian wants to kiss me?

BRIAN WANTS TO KISS ME???

"Only if you want to," he added, filling in my stunned silence.

"Yes!" I answered so intensely he rocked on his heels. "But only if *you* want to. But I don't want to pressure you, or—"

"No, I think we should—"

We were both talking at once and drifting closer together and I still couldn't believe this was happening. In my basement on Sunday, November 12, I was about to kiss my best friend, the boy I'd been crushing on for months.

This could be the greatest moment of my life. Or an epic disaster.

Brian shifted from foot to foot. "Should we be standing, or sitting?"

"I think this is fine?" I aimed for cool and confident, but my voice creaked like a rusty gate.

"OK. Um." He put a hand on my shoulder.

His throat bobbed as he swallowed. My pulse was drumming through my skin.

"Are you totally sure?" *Ugh, I wish my voice wasn't so shaky.* "I don't want you to regret it, or feel weird about it, or like you have to, or . . ." I forced myself to take a breath. "You're my best friend, and I don't want that to change."

"It won't. I promise." For a second, he gave me a look of determination. "And I'll try not to eat your face."

I couldn't help it. I started giggling. So did he, and we dissolved into a puddle of nervous laughter. I wondered if we'd ruined the moment, but when I caught my breath, Brian was still looking at me. He'd laughed so hard he had tears on his cheeks, and I reached up and brushed one away. He drew in a breath but didn't move.

So I kissed him.

Our lips touched. I closed my eyes. I went electric all over, like every nerve ending in my body was playing the guitar solo from "Bohemian Rhapsody."

I put my arms around him—

And he leaned away.

Cue record scratch.

I opened my eyes. The look on his face told me instantly. "Oh."

Brian was blushing. "Sorry. It wasn't bad! I kind of liked it."

It was exactly like Brian to be sorry that he couldn't give me what I wanted.

"But it wasn't 'Bohemian Rhapsody,'" I mumbled.

"Uh . . . what?"

"Never mind." I flopped onto the couch.

I couldn't be too disappointed, right? He'd tried. Not many guys our age would kiss another boy unless they were a hundred percent sure. Brian tried so hard for me. He was closing the door in the kindest way possible. But a piece of my heart was pinned in there, so it still hurt.

He sat beside me. "It was kind of nice. Honestly! And I'm really glad you're the first person I ever kissed."

"Me too." And I meant it. I was glad Brian was my first kiss, even if . . .

Even if it hurt a little.

Maybe more than a little.

It was too early for bed and the air felt too charged to keep talking, so I turned on the second half of the Raptors game. Five minutes in, Brian side-eyed me.

"'Bohemian Rhapsody'?"

I pressed a couch cushion over my face and groaned.

"Which part? Because if it was the verse where he tells his mom he killed a man and wishes he'd never been born—"

Now I was laughing. "No! The guitar solo, where Brian May is all, *Dun-dun-dun deedilly deedilly*—"

I played air guitar and Brian head-banged and just like that, it felt less weird.

Well, less weird for us. Brian and I were still plenty weird. We were the Weirdo Alliance.

When we finished, we slouched back into the couch and Brian put his arm around me. I could have told him he didn't have to do that, but I knew what he'd say. So I rested my head on his shoulder instead.

It wasn't romantic. It was . . . nice.

Nice wasn't 'Bohemian Rhapsody.' But when you kissed your best friend who wasn't actually into you, it could end much worse than *nice*.

"I love you, Ezra," Brian said.

I understood how he meant it. "I love you too," I said.

And I did. No matter what else I felt, I loved him like he loved me: He was the person who made me laugh, who made me feel relaxed, who I could tell virtually anything. My best friend.

I could accept that. I used to have feelings for my friend Colby and—

Never mind. Bad example.

But Brian wasn't Colby, and I was different now too. I could move on. I thought.

When the game was over, we got ready for bed. I switched off my lamp, and stared at my ceiling.

"Ezra?" Brian said. "We're cool, right?"

"Yeah."

"OK." He paused. "It's just . . . you're being really quiet. I'm the quiet one, remember?"

"I'm sleepy. We're cool, Brian. I promise."

I was telling the truth.

I hoped.

3. FIVE EASY STEPS TO SAVE THE DAYS

BRIAN

I thought kissing Ezra might solve one mystery in my brain, but it just left me with more questions.

"Is it weird that I'm thirteen and not romantically interested in anyone?" I asked Gabe and Brittany in the dairy aisle.

Brittany did most of her family's grocery shopping, since her mom died a year ago and her dad was a disaster in the kitchen apparently. My mom didn't love the grocery store either, so I tagged along sometimes and did our shopping. I liked any excuse to hang out with Gabe and Brittany, and Brittany was a tactical genius, so she helped me out. Plus, it was fun when we rolled up to a new cashier, three teenagers with two full carts, and they stared at us like we were pulling a prank.

Brittany grabbed two tubs of half-price yogurt and put one in my cart. "No, it's not weird. Movies make it seem like boys are all walking tornadoes of hormones, but it's perfectly normal not to be like that. What brought this on?"

"I kissed Ezra last Sunday."

They gave me a *whoa* look. I kept going. "I thought we should try, so I could be sure, but I didn't feel what Ezra felt. What if I never feel that way about anyone? There's no one else I want to kiss or anything. I wish I *did* like Ezra, because he's the best, and it would be so easy. But he'll fall in love with another guy someday, and maybe you two will get married, and what if that never happens for me? What if I end up alone? Like a cat lady, only I don't like cats. What if I become an iguana guy? What if I die alone and my iguanas break out of their tank and eat my corpse?"

Gabe and Brittany were staring at me. Gabe bit his lip to keep from laughing.

I tucked my hands in my pockets. "Sorry. That was a major anxiety dump."

Brittany frowned. "Did you have caffeine today?"

"Yeah, Kevan and I got iced cappuccinos after school."

She *tsked*. "You should stick to tea. Too much caffeine messes with your head."

Gabe set his hands on my shoulders. "What I'm hearing is that you still have abandonment issues, my man. But your friends aren't all going to ditch you, and there's only a slim chance lizards will eat you when you die."

A woman with a baby in her cart overheard that part. She shot us a horrified look and hurried toward the cheese.

"Also, let's go easy on the domestic stereotypes," Brittany said. "Single people can have fulfilling lives. You could go on plenty of adventures by yourself."

"That's true," Gabe said. "Although you don't have to go on adventures alone. You could wait and bring your tall, muscular boyfriend. He can carry things. He's very handy."

Brittany rolled her eyes. "Gabe, really? *Now?*"

Gabe folded his arms. My awkward tension meter tingled. "Wait. Are you two having a fight?"

Gabe sighed. "Not exactly. Brittany's thinking about taking next year off to travel—which is totally cool," he added as her glare intensified. "I just wish we were doing it together."

"But you're going to have college basketball," Brittany said. "That's *your* dream, and it's also cool. We'll have lots of time for adventures together. We can still be two independent people."

"I *know* that. I'm not trying to be jealous or controlling. Honestly, it's . . ." Gabe stopped. His shoulders slumped.

Brittany's face softened. "Oh." She touched Gabe's arm.

Suddenly it hit me: Gabe's dad had been in the military, and he'd died overseas. Gabe was worried about Brittany going away.

All three of us were a little scarred. That's why I didn't mind telling Gabe and Brittany my weirdest thoughts. They understood me too.

Brittany put an arm around Gabe, then she held her other arm out to me, and I joined the hug.

"The point is, maybe you'll have romantic feelings someday, or maybe you won't, and either way, it's OK," she said. "That's the case for lots of people. But you have time to figure out what's right for you. Don't add it to your list of worries. That's long enough already."

They let me go, and we steered our carts toward the checkout.

"How's Ezra doing with all this?" Brittany asked.

"I think he's OK. We still hang out like normal."

Gabe nodded. "Ezra's a good dude."

Gabe and Brittany made me feel better, as always. But as we waited in line, I started thinking about next year, when they'd be at college or off traveling the world. They were already busier now that they were seniors. They wouldn't always be around to take care of me. And then I started thinking about Ezra. He swore we were cool, but my anxiety hyperdrive was trying to convince me that his jokes felt more forced, and he looked away quicker when we made eye contact, and maybe he was pretending he was fine but I actually broke his heart and ruined everything.

"Hey." Brittany poked my shoulder as we were leaving the store. "Stop thinking so much and eat a half-price lemon bar."

I reached into the package she was holding open and took one. "It was that obvious?"

"I know you," she said.

Yes, you do, I thought as I bit into my lemon bar, and it calmed my brain for a while.

My next nightmare didn't involve being eaten by iguanas, although I wished it had. That would have been less terrifying. Instead, I dreamed about a witch who kidnapped children to steal their livers, and Richie was her latest victim. I jolted awake at four A.M.

At least it was Saturday, so I wasn't losing sleep on a school night. (Looking for the positive in a bad situation was another Dr. Bender tip.) After I went to pee, I hovered outside Mom's room for a minute, making sure everything sounded peaceful in there. I knew it was silly, but I still did it. The nightmares were about her, even when they weren't.

Dr. Bender called it post-traumatic stress. I didn't just lose Dad to jail in June; I almost lost Mom too. When Dad left, she'd broke down and taken a bunch of pills. I had to call 911. She'd ended up in the hospital, and Richie and I had to spend a month in foster care. Dr. Bender said it was natural that I wouldn't just get over something like that. The nightmares were like aftershocks. When Mom had first come home from the hospital, it took two weeks before I could sleep all through the night without checking on her. I'd been an exhausted bundle of panic attacks. It was super.

I peeked into Richie's room next. He was sprawled on his back, breathing steadily. Then I double-checked that the doors were locked before I went back to bed and began an argument I always lost.

Brian versus Brian, Round 4,576
Me: Everyone's fine. Let's go back to sleep.
Also Me: Come on. You know how this works.
Me: This is ridiculous! Richie's exactly where he was one minute ago. He's safe.
Also Me: Of course he is. But that doesn't matter. You can pretend this time will be different, or you can save half an hour and give up now.

With a sigh, I wrapped myself in my blanket and walked back to Richie's room. He didn't stir. I could have dragged him into the backyard by his ankles and he'd still have slept 'til morning. As I carved out a spot in the clothes and LEGO on his floor, I told myself I'd stay for just five minutes, until my anxiety hyperdrive cooled off.

I woke up to Richie hovering over me, the morning sun framing him in a halo of light.

"Good morning, sweetie," he said. "What was it this time?"

"You don't want to know."

"I always want to know."

"A witch was cutting out your liver."

"Wicked. How do you come up with this stuff?"

I wish I knew. Maybe then I could learn how to turn it off.

Richie reached out a hand like he was going to help me up. But instead, he stepped on my stomach.

"You *turd*," I gasped.

He took off, earning a five-step head start. But there weren't many places to hide in our little bungalow, and Mom was in the bathroom already. We circled the kitchen before I took him down in the living room. I had him pinned when Mom appeared.

"I thought maybe the house was on fire, the way you two were thundering around." She wrinkled her nose. "You couldn't have put on pants before going beast mode?"

"It's Saturday," Richie said from beneath me. "We don't need pants."

Mom muttered something about boys and clothes and testosterone. She gave us each a kiss on the cheek before she left to catch the bus. Mom had a job now, one of a million things that had changed in Life Part II. She was out a lot of afternoons and Saturdays running workshops at the Community YMCA for newcomers to Nova Scotia. She liked it, and it was good for her, though she'd get annoyed if I said the second part out loud. She reminded me that she was still the parent in the house whenever she thought I was worrying too much.

Richie and I toasted Eggos and hung out in our boxers playing video games, the same way we did most Saturday mornings. Richie helped keep me loose and distracted me from worrying that we might be doomed. See, I had this bad habit of reading research about kids like us. Late-night Internet searches were a dangerous thing.

Scientific Evidence Pointing to My Doom
1. Kids with an incarcerated parent are statistically more likely to have behavior problems, mental health issues, and legal troubles of their own.
2. Ditto for kids who spend time in foster care.
3. Have a parent with a mental illness? You guessed it.
4. Childhood trauma (like watching your mom nearly die) is extremely not ideal.

We were basically the definition of *at-risk kids*. If you caught us on a bad day—Richie scruffy-haired and scowling, me dark-eyed after a sleepless night—we could be cover models for some tragic brochure about youth in need.

We did have a few things going for us, though. We were only in care for a month, and we spent two of those weeks with Mrs. Clelland and Gabe. And let's be honest: It also didn't hurt that we were white. Another depressing fact I learned online was that Black kids in Nova Scotia were more likely to get suspended at school and stopped by police, had a harder time finding a job, and made less money even when they did. So Gabe, Ezra, and Ty, the best guys I knew, all had extra obstacles because the world was broken.

But I couldn't solve systemic racism on my own, and I should focus on what I *could* control (yep, Dr. Bender).

So I made a plan. I wrote it down and everything. If I was organized, maybe I could keep my family and my future on track.

Five Easy Steps to Save the Days*
1. Help Mom stay healthy
2. Keep Richie on track
3. Rule the eighth-grade honor roll
4. Improve social skills
5. Become a basketball star
*I know this is a terrible pun and I don't care

Dr. Bender would have raised her eyebrows at the first two, since they weren't totally in my control. Back when I saw her every week, we'd talked about how I wasn't responsible for my parents or my brother. But I could get groceries, do chores, and help Richie with his homework. If everything ran smoothly and Richie was happy, Mom would be less stressed, and it felt less likely she'd have another Incident. It was working so far.

(I also counted Mom's pills every week to make sure she was taking exactly the right amount. She'd have freaked if she knew I was doing it, but I couldn't help it.)

The last three were up to me. The work part of school had always been easier than the social part, but I was getting better. My SAWS still flared up sometimes, but I had three friends, and last week I made an actual joke in social studies. People laughed. It felt amazing.

I played basketball or shot around by myself almost every day, because exercise was good for my brain, and it gave me something to focus on. And between all my practice and my growth spurt, I'd improved a ton since last year. My goal was to get a starting spot on the team this year. If I did well at school and sports, I had a better shot at a college scholarship. That seemed like a long ways away still, but a kid like me had to be focused to beat the odds. So I worked hard. Except on Saturday mornings.

"I'm crushing you," Richie crowed as he whooped me in *Mario Kart* again. "Want to play *Minecraft* instead?"

"Sure."

He switched games, and we worked on building a new world together until the doorbell rang.

"Come in!" Richie yelled.

"We're not dressed," I reminded him.

He shrugged. "It's only Leo and Kevan."

The door opened, and two seconds later Kevan and his brother, Leo, Richie's best friend, were in our living room.

"I was going to put on pants," I told Kevan.

"It's all good," he said. "Remember how uptight you used to be? It feels like progress that you'll have me over when you're in your underwear."

"That was actually one of my milestones in therapy," I joked, and Kevan laughed, and I realized he was right. When I was with my friends, I remembered how far I'd come from shy loner Brian. I guess my plan was working.

4. CARTOON CRUSH

EZRA

"What's your deal? You're mopey," my sister, Nat, told me through my laptop speakers.

"I'm not mopey," I said.

"Well, you're less bouncy than usual."

"I'm never *bouncy*."

"Touchy, too." A thousand miles away, Nat peered at me on her phone like she was studying a bug through a magnifying glass. "Is this a puberty thing? Are you experiencing hormonal rage, Ezzy? That's normal for a boy your age. Don't be embarrassed. Embrace your body."

I rolled my eyes. Nat was ten years older than me, and technically my half sister from Dad's first marriage, though we didn't get hung up on stuff like that. She was great, except when she leaned into obnoxious big sister mode.

She waved. "Hello? You're thinking about the kiss, right? Do you want to skip the part where you pretend you're over it and admit it's bothering you?"

I flopped on my bed with my laptop propped against my knees. "It's been a whole week, Nat. I want a pill so

I can stop thinking about Brian like *that* and just be friends. There must be a formula that some famous white lady sells on her Instagram. With essential oils, or beet juice."

"What you need is a project," Nat said. "Channel all that angst into your music. Or basketball. That starts soon, right?"

"First tryout's on Tuesday. Then I'll be spending even more time with Brian. And he's extra cute in his jersey and shorts."

"Oh." Nat twisted a strand of hair around her finger. "Maybe you should talk to him again. You know, about what you're feeling."

I groaned. "Why? I don't want to make him feel bad."

Nat bit her lip, like she was gearing up for a lecture on honesty or something, but instead, she said, "What *do* you want?"

It was an annoying question, because it would be ridiculous to say *I want Brian to magically discover he has feelings for me.* "I just want things to be cool, I guess. And I want to master this Vampire Weekend song I'm working on in guitar lessons. Want to hear it?"

"We're changing the subject, huh? Real subtle." Nat laughed. "I actually have to go, Ezzy. But be good. Don't do drugs."

She blew me a kiss, then she was gone.

Ty and I lived a few blocks south of school, and Brian and Kevan lived in the same neighborhood to the north, so we met up by the basketball court outside most mornings. On Monday, I had a weird flutter in my chest as Brian and Kevan approached. It was a rare weekend where we didn't hang out at all, and my conversation with Nat was still buzzing in my head. I tucked my hands in my pockets because I suddenly wasn't sure what to do with them.

Should I give Brian a high five? A hug? Is that too much? Why have I forgotten how to act like a regular person?

Ty greeted Kevan and Brian with a clasped-hand, one-shoulder bump, so I did the same.

"You look tired," Ty said to Brian. "You stay up watching basketball or something?"

"Working on my science project," Brian replied, rubbing his eyes. "I think I know everything there is to know about the Bay of Fundy now."

"Seriously?" Kevan asked. "That's not due until Thursday. Don't be such a try-hard."

"It's all part of my system for success, Kev." Brian turned to me. "How was your weekend?"

"It was great!" That came out so much louder than I intended. Kevan and Ty gave me funny looks.

Suddenly Kevan grabbed my arm. "Whoa. Don't stare, but look who's coming."

Two guys were crossing the schoolyard. One was Colby. The other was taller than the last time I'd seen him and had grown a head of shaggy black hair, but we all recognized him.

"Victor MacLennan? Huh." Ty leaned against the fence. "I heard he moved."

"I heard a *lot* of things," Kevan said. "I didn't think he'd be back."

We stopped talking and struck casual *we're definitely not staring* poses as they passed. Kevan said "what's up" to Colby.

"Hey," Colby said. "Hey, Ty. Hey, Ezra."

"Hey," I said.

Victor gave us the slightest nod. Then they moved on.

We all turned to Brian.

He went red. "What? I'm not worried about Victor."

"Good," Ty said. "You shouldn't be."

Brian and Victor had a history. Last year, Victor had picked on Brian until Brian punched him in the face. Stuff like that made people go wild in junior high. When Victor didn't show up in September, rumors flew all over the place. But I guess he was back now.

"I wonder what his story is," Ty said.

"I bet Colby knows," Kevan said.

There was a time I could have asked Colby. We used to be best friends.

But we hadn't really talked since last June. That was also the last time I saw Victor. I went to Colby's house trying to figure out why Colby and I weren't getting along, and I told him I was gay. Victor overheard the whole thing.

Whatever. Coming out helped me learn who my real friends were, and I had three great ones right here.

The bell rang. Brian, Ty, and I headed to homeroom. Victor wasn't there, which didn't surprise me. Our principal, Ms. Floriman, knew better than to put Brian and Victor together again.

As much as I didn't want to, I thought about Colby and Victor all morning. At least it was a distraction from thinking about Brian, but it wasn't much better.

My friends knew Colby ghosted me after I came out to him, but I'd never mentioned that Victor was there too. I didn't really know why. I just didn't. Victor had been surprisingly chill about it—better than Colby—but it still felt strange that he was one of the first people to know.

I didn't hide who I was anymore. On the first day of eighth grade, I wore a T-shirt that said *Human* in rainbow letters. But it wasn't like I announced my sexuality at a school assembly. Straight kids didn't have to do that, so why should I?

Besides, I was used to people not knowing how to figure me out. Sometimes I got funny looks when someone tried to match my Polish last name, Komizarek, with my brown skin and curly hair. Or when I was out with just Dad, who's white. Mom reminded me that I never owed anyone an explanation about who I was, so I didn't sweat it . . . most of the time.

We walked to Kevan's house at lunch, and when we were huddled in his kitchen, he raised his hand dramatically. "I have an update. Victor's in my homeroom, and he didn't say a word. He whispered to Colby, but he didn't talk otherwise. He mostly just stared out the window. He's all broody now, like Zuko in *Avatar*."

"Mmm, Broody Zuko."

Yikes. It slipped out, and I instantly regretted it. Kevan choked back his laughter.

Ty patted my arm. "Ignore him, Ezra. There's no shame in crushing on an *Avatar* character. I've watched every Suki episode five times." He turned to Brian. "Biggest cartoon crush. Go."

Brian turned pink. "Um . . ."

"When I was six, I wanted to marry Doc McStuffins," Kevan admitted.

Ty pointed at him. "See? It's normal for Ezra to be hot for the prince of the Fire Nation."

What was hot right now was my entire face.

Kevan shrugged. "I guess. Broody does seem to be your type."

He looked from me to Brian and flashed a wicked grin. I kind of wanted to kill him. But Brian laughed, so I guess he wasn't embarrassed, and I tried not to make it weird.

Still, I owed Kevan a good burn. As we headed back to school, I was thinking of comebacks. It was better than thinking about Victor.

5. THE RISE OF SPICY B

BRIAN

The best thing about November was the start of basketball. Last year, I was a nervous wreck before tryouts, but now I knew I was good enough to make the team—another encouraging sign of how much I'd changed. I wasn't surprised to see my name on the team list outside the gym the morning after the last tryout, but it still felt good. Ty's and Ezra's names were there too.

"Return of the sizzle squad," Ty said happily. "It's going to be a good year."

Eighth grade was already better than seventh, but basketball made me *want* to go to school. I liked our new coach, Coach Williams. He started teaching P.E. this year after our old teacher retired. He was young, only a few years removed from playing college basketball. Ty kept begging him to show us if he could dunk, but he always shook his head and said, *"Don't want to break the rim."* He was the kind of coach you could joke around with.

After our fourth practice, Coach called me over as I was leaving the locker room.

"I want to talk to you about our exhibition game on Thursday," he said. "I'm starting you at point guard."

My grin was so big I could feel my cheeks stretching. "Really? I mean, uh, thanks, Coach."

"You've earned it, Brian. You see the court so well. Just remember: Being point guard means you set the pace for the team. We've got some great players and big personalities on this team, so I'm counting on you to be a leader."

My grin shrunk a little. "Right."

Coach chuckled. "I know you're quiet, and that's OK. Leaders don't have to be loud. But they choose their moments to be heard."

"OK, Coach. I'll try."

My mind was racing as I left the gym. Starting at point guard was a dream come true, but being a leader? *Me?* I was nothing like Andre, a ninth grader who was our team captain, or Ty, who was our best scorer, or even Ezra, who cracked jokes and made us feel like a team.

But I guess I needed to add it to my list: *Become a leader.*

Ty and Ezra were waiting for me in the hall.

"What was that about?" Ezra asked.

My grin crept back. "I'm starting at point guard on Thursday."

Ty scooped me up in a massive bear hug. "I knew it! Way to go, Spicy B!"

"Spicy B?" I wheezed as he nearly flattened my ribs.

He let me go. "That's your baller nickname. I've decided. You like spicy food, you have cayenne-pepper hair—" Ty rubbed my still-sweaty head. "And your game is spicy."

The night before our first game, Gabe took me to the Canada Games Centre and we spent an hour on ball-handling and shooting. Gabe said he got something out of our workouts, though I knew he could be doing this with his high-school teammates instead. I appreciated that he still made time for me.

When we were done, he beckoned me to a bench and pulled up a video of NBA bloopers on his phone. Steph Curry botching a dunk. Russell Westbrook losing his dribble. LeBron James whipping a pass into the stands. I half chuckled, half cringed through the whole thing.

"These guys are the best in the world, but they still make mistakes," Gabe said.

I wiped my face on my T-shirt. "Is this a life lesson?"

"You bet." Gabe nudged my shoulder. "You're good, Brian. You're smart, you work hard, and you're a wicked shooter. But you'll be *great* once you quit worrying about missing. Don't be afraid to screw up."

Gabe knew me too well. "You're almost as good as Dr. Bender. You could do this for a living."

He stretched. "I'm thinking about studying psychology in university actually. There aren't a lot of Black therapists around. Maybe I could help some people."

"Well, you can keep practicing on me. I need all the help I can get."

He shook his head. "Come on." He rose and pulled me to my feet.

On game day, I went to the bathroom at lunch, and again in last-period French, and again before I headed to the locker room. My stomach went wobbly when I was anxious. I called it the ARPs: anxiety-related pooping. I always got the ARPs before games. I confessed this to Gabe once, and he'd told me that NBA legend Bill Russell, who'd won eleven championships, used to throw up before games. So it could have been worse.

"Don't be afraid to make mistakes," I whispered in the end stall of the first-floor bathroom.

Someone at the urinals snickered. "You OK in there?"

Oh no. I thought I was alone. I sat perfectly still until I was sure they'd gone.

When I made it to the gym, I changed into my uniform with the number thirteen on the back. Parents showed up to watch, and a few teachers, including Gabe's mom, Mrs. Clelland. She was the best teacher I'd ever had, and she'd taken Richie and me in for a while when we needed a place to stay, so she was more than a teacher to me. She gave me a big *I'm proud of you* smile from her place in the stands.

As I took my spot before tipoff, I couldn't help thinking about who wasn't here to see me start for the first time: my dad.

The referee tossed the jump ball, and Ty tipped it back to me. Game on.

We had a good team, and it showed. St. Agnes didn't have anyone big or quick enough to stop Ty and Andre. I tried to focus on making good passes and playing defense. I scored my only two points of the half when I stole the ball from the St. Agnes point guard and raced to the rim for a layup.

"Spicy B!" Ty yelled.

By halftime, we had a twelve-point lead. Coach Williams called me over during the break.

"You're playing great," he said. "Now shoot more. I want at least three shots in the third quarter."

I blinked. "Even if I miss?"

"Doesn't matter. Three shots."

St. Agnes started the second half with the ball. We forced them into a miss, and I dribbled up the court. My defender dropped back to prevent an easy pass to Ty or Andre.

I glanced at the bench. *Shoot*, Coach mouthed. So I did.

The ball looped around the rim and fell out. But it landed in Ty's hands, and he got fouled trying to lay it in. He made both his free throws.

I waited two trips down the floor before I shot again. It clanked off the rim and bounced to St. Agnes.

"Good look, Brian," Coach called. "Keep shooting."

Next time I had the ball, I made eye contact with Ty, and he popped out to set a screen on my man to get me open. Ty's defender was slow in switching, so I drove to the basket. As I jumped, Ty's man lunged at me. I wrapped a one-handed pass around his back, right into Ty's hands as he rolled to the hoop for an easy layup.

He fist-bumped me on the way down the court. "Great dish, Spicy B."

"You're really trying to make that stick, huh?"

"I told you, it's your official nickname."

A minute later, Coach subbed Ezra in for me. Ezra high-fived me as I headed to the bench.

"Sorry I only took two shots," I told Coach. "I was going to shoot the third one, but Ty was open."

Coach laughed. "Brian, that was the slickest pick and roll I've seen in a minute. You did exactly what I wanted. Even your first miss got us two points on Ty's rebound." He tapped his temple. "I love how you see the floor and get everyone involved. But when you're in attack mode, that makes the defense react and opens up our offense even more. Keep it up."

He sent me back in with six minutes left and our lead at fifteen. My defender sagged off me, so I pulled up behind the three-point line and shot.

Swish.

That one felt good.

Ezra yelled, "Spicy B for THREEEEE!" and all the guys on the bench echoed, "Spicy BEEEEE." So I guessed the nickname was happening. I liked it.

6. THE LEAST ROMANTIC PLACE EVER

EZRA

The locker room was loud and goofy after we finished off St. Agnes. Jayden Grouse stood on a bench with his shirt off and dropped a freestyle rap about our win, while Ty and I drummed on the bench to give him a beat.

Jayden pointed at Brian. *"Shout out to Spicy B, he lights it up from three. He loves to pass to Ty, but he should give the rock to me!"*

Everyone cracked up, and Brian turned red.

"You were smooth out there, B," Andre said.

"Thanks," Brian said.

Andre shook his head. "You're so low-key. You can get hyped sometimes, you know."

Brian shrugged. "I like to let my game do the talking."

Everyone laughed again, and Brian grinned.

"Respect Spicy B's chill," Ty said. "He doesn't show off when he makes one shot, like that number fifteen on St. Agnes."

Andre snickered. "Yeah, he had a lot to say when he scored on Harrison."

Everyone razzed Harrison Kinney, a big ninth grader who was the only guy taller than Ty.

Harrison scowled. "That kid was talking trash all game. He's a little—" Then Harrison said an ugly slur. One that felt like a punch in the stomach.

I froze. A weird feeling of shame washed over me, even though I didn't do anything wrong. Harrison hadn't been talking about me, but I still felt awful.

I should say something.

Brian beat me to it. "Um. Harrison, that's not OK."

Everyone went quiet, probably out of shock that Brian spoke up.

Harrison's jaw tensed. "I was just joking. I didn't mean it like . . . you know."

Ty stood up. "It doesn't matter how you meant it. It's not OK. Don't ever say that again, got it?"

"Jeez, what's the big deal? I—" Harrison's eyes landed on me and my rainbow T-shirt. His mouth fell open. "Oh. Ezra. I didn't, um, are you . . . ?"

I wanted to disappear. But I couldn't, so I decided to make a joke. "The hottest guy here, by a mile? Thank you for noticing." Andre snickered, and the tension eased a little. "And yeah, I'm gay."

Welp. Guess I'm out to the whole team. Thanks, Harrison.

Ty glared around the room. "No one has a problem with that, right?"

"Nah. Ezra's cool." Andre slid over and offered his fist. I gratefully gave him a fist bump. No one was going to argue with Ty and Andre. Not out loud, anyway.

Harrison went pale. "Ezra, I'm sorry. I'm not prejudiced or anything. Honest." He swallowed hard. "You won't tell Coach, will you?"

Anger buzzed in my chest. Maybe Harrison was sincere, but he mostly seemed worried that I'd get him in trouble. I hadn't even thought about that, but now I considered it for just a second . . .

Yeah, I could tell Coach, or even Ms. Floriman. Maybe Harrison would be suspended from the team. But I didn't want that, and I didn't want teachers to rally around me and make a big deal of it. I just wanted to be *me*. I wanted to goof around in the locker room without anyone caring who I like or saying gross slurs.

I straightened my glasses. "I won't. Just learn some new words, OK? And don't use *gay* as an insult, either."

"I won't." He held out his hand. "Are we good?"

I guess I was supposed to let it go and move on, like when I shrugged off strange looks or clueless comments from white people. And it wasn't like I wanted to hold a grudge; I just wished Harrison had known better already so that I didn't have to deal with this. But I shook his hand.

The locker room was quieter now. No more jokes. I cleared my throat.

"Just so you know, I'm not crushing on any of you. Especially not in here. The locker room is the least romantic place ever. It smells like armpits and feet."

Jayden snickered. "Look, if you want to admire the eight-pack from a distance, I'm not even mad." He flexed his stomach.

"Your abs are great," I shot back. "But that eight-pack of chin hairs you refuse to shave isn't helping you."

"Ouch!" Andre hollered.

Ty pulled out his phone. "Hello, 911? I'd like to report a murder."

Laughter rippled around the room. Even Jayden smiled. "It's like that, huh?"

As he left the locker room, he lightly punched my shoulder. So did Andre. I felt better knowing they weren't going to treat me differently. Then Harrison mumbled one more *sorry* on his way out, and I had to bite back a sigh.

Brian and Ty waited with me until everyone else had left. I knew they were doing it to protect me. A lump built in my throat, and I went to the sink to splash cold water on my face.

Brian followed me. "You OK?"

I dried my face. "Yeah. It's fine. Thanks for sticking up for me."

Ty shook his head. "It's not fine. You shouldn't have to hear stuff like that. I know most guys on the team are cool, but Andre and I will make sure no one gives you any trouble or spreads any rumors."

"Honestly, Ty, I don't care who knows anymore."

I meant it. I think. But it wasn't like I suddenly felt brave. I was just done with worrying about what I said, or who I looked at for too long, or what people were thinking about me. I was tired.

The streetlights were glowing against the dimming gray sky when we left. Soggy brown oak leaves clung to the edge of the sidewalk. In November, the trees always looked so naked and sad.

That's kind of poetic. I should use that in a lyric.

"What song is that?" Brian asked.

"Huh?"

"You were humming."

"Oh." I hummed a lot when I was thinking. It was kind of embarrassing when people caught me doing it in public, but Kevan insisted it was part of my dreamy rock star vibe and I should go with it. "Nothing, really."

Ty mimed a jump shot. "You know, our team's going to be great this year. Ezra, you bring the sizzle off the bench, Brian's unleashing his spiciness—"

"I still can't believe you made that nickname stick." Brian grinned.

"Sizzle and Spice," I said. "We should be a rap duo. Like Salt-N-Pepa."

"I could never be a rapper," Brian said.

"Not true," Ty shot back. "You were spitting bars at my party last summer. I haven't forgotten about that."

"No one could ever forget," I said. "We know it's your dream to be the next Jay-Z, standing onstage in front of thousands of screaming fans."

Brian laughed. He gave me a shove, and I bumped into Ty. Ty nudged me back into Brian. I pinballed between them, then I threw an arm around each of their shoulders and jumped up. They were both taller than me, and my feet dangled above the ground. They carried me like that for half a block.

7. KABOOM

BRIAN

We won our second game in a blowout against Halifax Central. I scored twelve points this time, all on three-pointers. The guys yelled "Spicy B for three!" every time.

I was so excited to tell Dad about it that I was barely even nervous when we visited on the first Sunday in December. He smiled as he walked into the visiting room and pulled Mom and me into a hug. Pressed into his shoulder, I could tell he'd just showered and changed into a fresh blue jumpsuit. The smell of jail-standard detergent was burned into my memory now. I caught a whiff of it after practice one day when Harrison pulled a T-shirt out of his backpack and my brain instantly plunked me in this room. I'd almost asked him what detergent his family uses, but that was a weird thing to ask a guy when he was changing. Especially a guy like Harrison.

He was the only player on the team who wasn't very friendly with me, and I knew it was because I'd called him out. It wasn't obvious, just little things like avoiding eye contact or trying extra hard to block my shot if we were on opposite teams in practice. I knew I'd done the right thing, and I didn't regret it, but I also didn't like that one of my teammates was mad at me.

I pushed Harrison out of my mind. I had other things to think about.

"Richie's at the Sidhus'," I told Dad. He glanced at Mom, who bit her lip, and that was all we said about it.

I let Mom and Dad catch up and scrolled through my phone to try to give them a little privacy. When it was my turn, we talked about basketball. Dad gave my arm a playful punch when I told him about all my threes.

"I love it! Play with confidence, B-Man." His eyes went cloudy, but he covered it with a grin. "You'll have to teach your mother how to shoot video on your phone and bring me some clips next time."

Mom exhaled. "I haven't made it to a game yet."

"You haven't?" Dad's face fell. "*Julia*. It's important."

"It's fine," I said quickly. "Mom's working full-time now, and it's going great. Right, Mom?"

Dad let it drop, but suddenly my anxiety hyperdrive kicked in. They were both feeling guilty that I was the kid with absent parents.

When it was time to go, Dad whispered, "I'm proud of you, B-Man" in my ear, and I had to clench my teeth so I didn't get teary.

Mom and I were quiet on the ride home until the bus turned toward the bridge.

"Does it bother you that I haven't come to see you play yet?" she asked.

I shook my head. "I've only had two games. It's not a big deal. Ezra's parents haven't come either."

"With their income, you'd think they could afford to take an afternoon off for their kid," Mom muttered. Then she sighed. "Sorry. That was mean." She stared out the rain-streaked window. "Sometimes I wish I could be the super-involved PTA mom who has her crap together, you know?"

Mom used a harsher word than "crap" though. Dad swore all the time, but Mom only swore when she was stressed. Keeping Mom un-stressed was a critical part of my survival plan.

"Mom, it's fine." I covered my mouth to stifle a yawn.

She tilted her head. "How late were you up last night? You seem tired lately."

"It wasn't that late. I'm fine." I stuck in my earbuds so we didn't have to talk anymore.

I hadn't stayed up late. But after I'd gone to bed, I'd started overthinking every interaction with Harrison, then I'd started doing the same with Ezra. Had I done enough after Harrison said that awful thing? Was Ezra still bummed about how I'd reacted after the kiss? We didn't talk about it anymore, and most of the time it seemed like we were OK, but sometimes things felt different. Or maybe that was me overthinking too. Then I'd started wishing that I could *like* him the way he liked me. I knew Brittany was right that it was fine I don't feel that way, but it would have been so much easier if I could live happily ever after with Ezra.

Well, I knew it wouldn't make everything easy. Ezra still dealt with ignorant people, obviously. But he knew who he was, and I admired that about him.

I didn't feel like telling any of this to Mom, but for a second I considered saying that I wouldn't mind seeing Dr. Bender again soon. It had been almost two months now. I'd seen her every week for a while, then we'd trailed off since I was doing a lot better—and since therapy wasn't cheap. But now that Mom had gone from casual to full-time at work, she got health benefits, so it probably wouldn't cost us as much.

Still, I didn't say anything. I knew she felt bad about working so much and spending less time with Richie and me. She didn't need to be worrying about my mental state too. And I was fine, really. It was just little stuff. It wasn't a big deal.

We got off the bus near Robie Street and headed in opposite directions. I was meeting Ezra, Ty, Kevan, and some other kids from school at Park Lane for a movie. Honestly, I felt like going home for a nap, but I didn't want to bail.

I boarded another bus toward Spring Garden Road. This one was full. And loud. A group of college-age guys were horsing around in the back, and the woman in front of me was having an angry conversation on her phone, and a man across the aisle kept coughing like he had two pounds of goo stuck in his throat. I closed my eyes and turned up my music, but my skin buzzed and my chest went tight.

No, I pled with my brain. *Not now.* But the explosion happened anyway.

KABOOM: HALIFAX TRANSIT EDITION
You're trapped There's no way out **Your mom is stressed** *Your plan isn't working* YOU HURT EZRA **You're supposed to be a leader, but Harrison is mad at you** *The theater will be crowded* Too many people *You'll be STUCK* You're not cut out for this *You need to be MORE and BETTER and STRONGER* You're not going to make it *You're not enough* You'll NEVER be enough

Sweat beaded on my forehead. It was hard to breathe. I tried to practice my grounding exercise, but every nerve in my body was screaming *Make it stop.* I'd had enough panic attacks that I knew what to expect and that they didn't last forever, but that didn't make them suck any less.

This was my first one since the second week of school. I was starting to hope I'd left them behind.

My stomach churned, and I knew it was a lost cause. I couldn't sit in a crowded theater. I couldn't even handle the bus anymore. I yanked the stop cord and wobbled out of my seat. The second the back doors opened, I rushed out and hunched over with my hands on my knees. Rain splashed the back of my neck. Focusing on the trickle of water running down my spine helped me settle down.

Then the moment passed, and I was cold and wet.

I sat on the bench in the bus shelter and sent a pathetic group text.

> Can't make it. Got delayed coming back from visiting dad. Sorry

It wasn't exactly a lie. I had gotten delayed, by my garbage brain.

Kevan: Bummer dude. We'll miss you
Ezra: Everything OK?
Me: Yeah catch you later

Well, that was kind of a lie. But if I told my friends what had happened, I'd ruin their afternoon. I didn't want them stressing out.

Besides, I *was* OK. This was only a blip. I just needed a nap.

With a sigh, I tucked my phone and my soggy transfer in my pocket and crossed the street to catch a bus home.

8. MOONLIGHT SONATA

EZRA

On the scale of great root beers, there was A&W root beer served in a frosted mug, and then there was everything else. When the movie ended, we flocked to the A&W in the basement of Park Lane for burgers.

"How fast do you think you could chug the whole thing?" Kevan asked, lifting his drink to Ty and me.

Madi Jacobs wrinkled her nose. "Why do boys always want to turn food into a contest?"

"Honestly, Kev. A true foodie takes the time to enjoy things." I took a slow sip of my root beer and let out an exaggerated *ah*.

Kevan gasped in offense. "No one understands good food better than me! You sure *enjoyed* all those cookies I smuggled into the theater."

Ty patted Kevan's head. "We know, Kev. They were delicious."

"Bet I could drink it in six seconds," Miranda Wong said. "Think you can beat that?"

Kevan stared at her in admiration. "Probably not, no."

Madi leaned forward. "I've been thinking. We should have a talent show at school."

"Like a root beer chugging contest?" Kevan asked.

Madi rolled her eyes. "No! An actual talent show!"

"So basically, you want to sing in front of the whole school," Miranda teased.

"A talent show would be great," I said. "You're a great singer, Madi."

She beamed at me. "You should play guitar too! You're amazing!"

Ty tapped his knuckles on the table. "I like this. Ezra needs a place to show off his skills. He's in. Right, Ezra?"

"I guess, yeah." I couldn't really say no, not with everybody looking at me. The idea of playing at school sounded terrifying . . . but maybe kind of fun too.

"I could do stand-up," Ty continued. "I've been saving up jokes about Mr. Harding's sweater vests since September."

"I'm sure Ms. Burtt would get the school band to play," Miranda said.

"I could bake stuff and sell it," Kevan said. "We could make it a fundraiser or something."

"That's a great idea! If we raise money for the school music program, Ms. Burtt will definitely say yes." Madi turned to me. "Let's talk to her tomorrow at lunch."

I blinked. "How come you're all volunteering me for stuff?"

"Because you have excellent leadership potential, Citizen Komizarek," Ty offered in a dead-on impression of

Ms. Virth, our social studies teacher. Everyone cracked up. Ty was going to be great at comedy. "But save the show until March, after basketball season," he added. "We need to stay focused if we want to win the title this year."

"I guess we could wait 'til then," Madi agreed. "That would give us time to get organized and get people to sign up."

Miranda swiped three of Kevan's fries. "I always forget you're artsy *and* sporty," she said to me.

I pressed my palms together. "I am a complex soul."

"You're weird," Miranda said. "That's good. Weird is interesting."

Kevan slid his fries away from Miranda. "Am I interesting?"

"You're a good baker and kind of funny." Miranda darted her hand in and snatched a few more fries. "But I'm not into boys, so don't get any ideas."

Kevan shrugged. "Fair enough."

We tossed around more ideas for a talent show before we headed out. The more we talked about it, the more it sounded like fun.

I was halfway home when I thought to check in with Brian. It was a bummer he ended up missing the movie. I started a couple texts—one asking about his visit with his dad, then one about Madi's idea for a talent show—but I deleted both. I figured he maybe didn't want to talk about jail, and I didn't want to make him feel like he'd missed out on a good time.

I settled on writing, I bet you're bummed that you missed smelling the guys in front of us at the movies who took a bath in cheap colon

Ha I meant cologne but colon works too

Brian replied with a barfing emoji. I saw three dots like he was going to say something else, but then he disappeared.

Brian seemed quiet on Monday too, but I didn't get much chance to talk to him because Madi grabbed me at recess to prepare our pitch for the talent show. At lunchtime, we headed to the music room to find Ms. Burtt.

I didn't spend a lot of time in the music room, since I wasn't in band, but Ms. Burtt let me leave my guitar in here on days I had lessons after school, and I liked the vibe in here every once in a while.

Today, Ms. Burtt was at her desk, eating salad out of a plastic container. Band kids were scattered around the room. At the far end, a shaggy-haired kid with their back to us was playing the piano. I recognized the piece, something classical I'd heard around the house. My dad's favorite musical genre was bewigged dead dudes. The song was slow and haunting and kind of hypnotic. I was tempted to hang back and listen, but Madi was on a mission. She marched to Ms. Burtt's desk, and I followed. Before Ms. Burtt could even set down her fork, Madi launched into the whole pitch. Ms. Burtt's eyes lit up when Madi mentioned the fundraiser part.

"This is a great idea," she said. "I'll take it up with Ms. Floriman, but I'm sure she'll agree. There are so many talented kids in this school. It would be nice to give you all a place to shine."

"Great!" Madi beamed. "And we're happy to do all the organizing for it. Right, Ezra?"

"Uh, right." I wasn't sure what I'd gotten myself into, but I had a feeling that my part in organizing might be doing whatever Madi said.

"We're having a talent show?" A kid with a frohawk who was spinning on a drum stool piped up. "Can anyone join?"

"Sure," I said. "That's the point."

He grinned. "Cool. Can I play drums? I play percussion in band, which is fun and all, but Ms. Burtt hasn't picked any songs yet where I get to use a whole kit. I've been drumming since I was three. My dad and my uncles have a band, and I play with them sometimes."

"This is Caleb Drummond," Ms. Burtt offered. "He's in seventh grade. He's very energetic."

"And this is Nneka. They play bass." Caleb waved toward a kid with long twists in their hair who was eating rice from a container. Nneka nodded at me.

"Hey, Nneka, we should play together for the talent show!" Caleb exclaimed. He stopped spinning and looked back at me. "What do you play?"

"Ezra's a wicked guitar player."

I looked up. The kid at the piano had turned around. I

hadn't recognized him from behind now that his hair was long, but it was Victor.

"I saw you at your recital in June," he reminded me. He nodded at Madi. "You were great too."

Madi glared at Victor like she wanted to vaporize him with her mind. My mind spun while I tried to match everything I knew about Victor from last year with this guy who was hanging out in the music room, playing a gorgeous song on the piano.

"'Moonlight Sonata,'" I blurted out, as the name of the piece popped into my head.

Madi gave me a curious look.

Victor's lips curled in a tiny half grin. "You know your stuff."

"I didn't know you could play like that." I winced as the words left my mouth. Of course I didn't know he could play like that. I barely knew anything about him.

He shrugged. "Maybe I'll do the talent show too."

"That would be *great*." Madi's voice dripped with snark. "The talent show is open to anyone who is *committed* and won't just *disappear*."

The room went quiet.

"Awkward," Caleb said.

Ms. Burtt cleared her throat. "Why don't you see me tomorrow, Madi. I'll talk to Ms. Floriman at the end of the day, and—"

"Bro, there you are! You coming?"

Everyone turned. Colby stood in the doorway, skateboard tucked under his arm. He was in a hoodie and shorts, like always, because Colby was one of those guys who never wore pants, not even in December. He was looking at Victor, but he smirked when he noticed everyone staring.

"Did I interrupt something?" He nodded at me. "Hey, Ezra. Madi."

"Hey," I said. Madi exhaled a loud *hmph*.

"Yeah, I'm coming." Victor rose from the piano bench. Our eyes met as he passed, and he half smiled again before he ducked to avoid Madi, who was still working on telekinetic vaporization. As they headed down the hall toward the back exit, I heard the wheels of Colby's skateboard on the floor and Victor's footsteps picked up to keep pace.

"No riding in the halls!" Ms. Burtt called, but they were gone.

"Good riddance," Madi muttered.

I was curious why she couldn't stand Victor and Colby. She used to hang out with them all the time, since they were dating her two best friends—Colby with Jemma and Victor with Alicia. Obviously, something had changed though.

But that was in the back of my mind. Mostly I remembered when I was the one hurrying after Colby, trying to keep up.

I told Madi I'd see her later and found Ty and Kevan in the cafeteria. Ty gave me a high five when I shared that Ms. Burtt loved the talent show idea.

"We should film it," Kevan said. "We can put your performance online. Maybe it'll go viral."

"I don't want to be Internet famous, Kev." I glanced around. "Where's Brian?"

"He went home for lunch," Ty said.

"By himself?"

Kevan shrugged. "You know Brian."

When the bell rang, we headed to French. Brian slid in at the last second before Monsieur Belliveau started class. He only gave me a glance before he opened his binder.

"Everything OK?" I whispered.

"What? Yeah." He fiddled with his pen. "How did your, uh . . . your thing go?"

"Good. Ms. Burtt's on board for the talent show. But . . ." I almost mentioned how strange it was to find Victor playing the piano, but I stopped. Brian seemed distracted. Or maybe he didn't really want to talk.

Eventually he glanced up. "But what?"

"Oh, we still need Ms. Floriman's permission. But Ms. Burtt thinks she'll say yes."

"Yeah, probably."

He was still playing with his pen, eyes down. It felt like something he would have done a year ago, when he was too shy to talk much in school. But he hadn't been like that with me for a long time. I wanted to ask again if there was something bothering him—then heat filled my face as I wondered if *I* was bothering him. I kept trying to be chill since the kiss, even though I couldn't just turn off my feelings. But maybe he noticed and found it weird.

I was starting to think maybe Nat was right, and we should talk about it more. I wanted to ask him to come over after school. But when the bell rang at the end of the day, he mumbled a goodbye and took off without even waiting for Kevan.

When I got home, I plugged in my guitar and distracted myself by thinking about the talent show. I ran through a few favorite songs, thinking about what to play. If I was going to perform at school, I had to pick something good. But as I was running through riffs, my mind drifted again, bouncing between Brian and Victor and Colby.

When I fell asleep, I had the weirdest dream. I was supposed to play a concert, but Colby and Brian were driving me to the concert hall, and they kept getting lost. I was frustrated that we were going to be late and kept trying to give directions from the back seat, but Colby acted like he couldn't understand me, and Brian didn't say a word. Just when I was ready to give up, I was suddenly onstage with my guitar. But I was in my underwear.

And Victor was the only person in the audience. And he was in his underwear too.

Waking up was a relief. *It was only a dream*, I reminded myself. But it took a while to shake all the strange feelings that came with it.

9. OK/NOT OK

BRIAN

I was working on a math assignment when Mom knocked on my door, then burst right in. I bit back a sigh. *Why knock if you're not going to wait for an answer?*

"Dinner's ready," she said.

"Be there in a minute." I had two problems left, though I'd been staring at one for five minutes. Math was my toughest subject, but I usually didn't get this stuck. I usually didn't have this much homework, either. But it'd been harder to concentrate and get things done in class all week. Everyone was so loud. Maybe because we were close to the holiday break.

"Come eat, Brian. Your homework isn't going anywhere." Mom set a hand on my shoulder.

I shrugged her off. "I said *in a minute*. Leave me alone."

Mom drew a breath. A flash of guilt ran through me. I didn't know why I'd snapped like that.

Mom's brow furrowed as she sat on my bed. "Brian. Not every parent would say this—and I certainly wouldn't say it to Richie—but maybe you should ease up. You had a ninety-six average on your report card last week. And right now, I think you might be hangry. So take a break and come eat."

I sighed. "Fine."

Eating did help, though I didn't admit it out loud. I shoveled pasta into my mouth and barely heard a word until Richie poked me with his foot under the table.

I looked up. "What?"

Mom and Richie were both looking at me.

"I asked what you wanted for Christmas," Mom said.

Christmas. Ugh. I still needed to get gifts for Mom and Richie. I should get something for Ezra too. And Mrs. Clelland and Gabe, since they'd been so good to me—

"Brian? Is there anything you need for basketball? Or a new backpack, or—"

"I don't know, OK?" My cheeks flushed. Richie shot me a dirty look.

"Jeez, what's your problem?" he asked.

"*Richie,*" Mom scolded. She turned to me and hesitated. "Hey, it's been a while since you saw Dr. Bender. Maybe you should have a check-in."

There it was. Mom thought I should go back to therapy. Even though I'd had the same thought, somehow it felt worse coming from her.

I looked down at my plate. "Yeah, sure," I mumbled. "Maybe after Christmas. I'm OK right now."

Mom sighed but didn't push. I finished eating and hurried back to my room.

The next afternoon, my body was full of bees as I changed into my uniform for our last game before holiday break. I'd barely talked to anyone all day. Super Awkward Weirdo Syndrome had returned with a vengeance. I waited 'til my teammates left the locker room before I went to the sink and splashed water on my face. Then I had an argument with my reflection.

> *Brian versus Brian, Round 4,592*
> *Me: I'm OK.*
> *Also Me: You sure about that?*
> *Me: Mom and Richie are doing fine, my grades are great, and I'm the starting point guard on the school basketball team. My plan is working. I'm OK.*
> *Also Me: If you have to tell yourself you're OK, you're not OK.*

The fluorescent lights in our aging gym made me wince when I stepped out of the locker room. I was hyperaware of everything—the noise of the crowd, the worn white-and-green paint on the gym walls, the squeak of every sneaker. Usually, I settled down once I warmed up and my blood got pumping, but today, the bees didn't go away.

After Ty won the jump ball, I dribbled past my man and flung a pass to Andre in the corner. He launched a three-pointer that missed. I rushed toward the basket, grabbed the rebound, and shot. My defender slapped my arm as I released the ball, and the shot rolled off the rim.

I expected to hear the referee's whistle, but it didn't come. Fairview rebounded the ball and raced down the court.

"That was a foul," I barked at the ref as I hurried to catch up.

He gave me a silent stare. Ty tilted his head at me.

Nothing went right in the first quarter. Our shooting was cold. Our defense broke down and we gave up easy baskets. Five minutes into the quarter, Coach had seen enough and called timeout. His words faded into the crowd noise as I perched on the bench, one knee bouncing. My eyes drifted to the scoreboard: Fairview was up 18–8 already. We were embarrassing ourselves.

As the huddle ended, I was two steps onto the court before Coach called me back.

"Didn't you hear me? Ezra's in. I'm giving you a breather." He paused. "Are you doing OK, Brian? You don't seem like yourself today."

Heat spread across my face. I mumbled that I was fine and went back to the bench. Coach left me there for most of the second quarter. The team found a better rhythm without me, but we were still ten points down at halftime. During the break I got in as many shots as I could, trying to find a groove. But I missed my first shot of the third quarter. A few minutes later, I was guarding my man when I ran smack into the chest of another Fairview player. My man coasted to the hoop for a layup. Harrison collected the ball and inbounded it to me.

"Call the screens and help on defense," I seethed at him. "Don't stand there like a pylon next time."

"Man, chill out," he snapped back, which made me even madder.

The Fairview guard overheard us. "You can't stop me anyway," he crowed as he jogged downcourt.

Now I was boiling.

As I reached our three-point line, I shook him with a crossover dribble and sped past. He chased me down and fouled me from behind as I released my shot. The whistle blew, I tumbled to the floor, the ball rolled around the rim . . . and fell out.

I slapped the floor and swore.

The words flew out of my mouth—not just one, but a creative four-hit combo—before I realized I'd yelled loud enough for the whole gym to hear.

The referee blew his whistle again. "Technical foul on thirteen. No need for that kind of language, son."

Everyone was looking at me. My teammates covered their mouths, either in shock or because they were trying not to laugh. Half the Fairview players and kids in the stands were openly snickering. A few parents murmured. I was glad my mom wasn't around to watch.

But Mrs. Clelland was in the stands with Gabe and Brittany. I met her eyes as Ty helped me off the floor and then quickly looked away.

As we waited for Fairview to shoot a free throw for my technical foul, Ty put an arm around my shoulders. "What's up, B? You're ghost-pepper-level spicy today."

"I don't know," I mumbled. My adrenaline buzzed and my whole body was tingling. I didn't know why I was so *angry*. I hadn't even felt this fiery when I'd punched Victor back in June. It was freaking me out.

The Fairview player missed, then it was my turn to shoot two shots for the foul before my outburst. At the free-throw line, I bounced the ball three times, spun it in my hands, took a deep breath, and exhaled as I released.

I made both shots—the first thing I hadn't screwed up all game.

As the second shot dropped through the mesh, the whistle blew. I turned and saw Jayden coming in to replace me. I walked to the bench with my head down.

"I'm sorry, Coach," I murmured.

He stopped me. "I didn't take you out to punish you. I want to make sure you're all right."

The way he said it, like he was worried, made me wish he was mad instead.

"I just got frustrated. Six was talking trash, and I let it get to me. It won't happen again."

Coach let me go. I sat at the end of the bench and draped my warm-up shirt over my head to tune everything else out.

Someone plopped beside me. Without looking, I knew it was Ezra.

"What's going on?" he asked quietly.

"I wish people would stop asking that."

"Oh." Ezra's voice hitched. "Sorry."

I didn't mean to sound so harsh. I should have been the one to say sorry—not just for snapping at him. A guilt bomb went off in my brain. Ezra was always there for me, and I knew I'd broken his heart a little but I didn't know what to say, and I hadn't told him about my panic attack, and I'd basically been the worst friend. I should say sorry. But my throat was tight. I couldn't risk crying during a game.

Coach glanced my way at the start of the fourth quarter, but he didn't send me back in. He was probably worried I'd freak out again. Obviously, I wasn't leader material.

We lost by six points. I trudged out to shake hands with Fairview and murmur an apology to the referee. Then I rushed to the locker room.

The team changed in silence. It was our first loss, and we all knew we blew this one. I wasn't the only one in a funk, although my funk felt deep enough to swallow the whole room.

I was halfway dressed when Andre said, "Yo, B, I didn't know you could swear like that."

Jayden snickered. "I'd never heard all those words in that order before. I'm honestly impressed."

Everyone laughed. Despite myself, I cracked a smile. My teammates' jokes made it seem like less of a big deal, but I knew I'd never live it down. They'd tease me for the rest of the season.

Mrs. Clelland, Gabe, and Brittany were waiting for me outside the locker room. They offered me a ride home. I told them I could walk, but Mrs. Clelland insisted.

"It's pouring out."

"You'll never win this argument with Mom," Gabe chimed in. "Just accept it."

I gave in. Mrs. Clelland wasn't kidding; the rain was falling in sheets, and we got drenched as we scrambled to her car. Gabe sat in back with me.

I could tell they wanted to talk, so as Mrs. Clelland pulled out of the parking lot, I got the jump on the lecture.

"I'm sorry I swore," I said. "It was an accident. It won't happen again."

She caught my eye in the rearview mirror. "Brian, I'm not upset about that."

The buzz in my chest returned. I couldn't wait to get out of this car. I wanted to be away from everybody.

I never felt that way around Gabe and Brittany. *What is wrong with me?*

Gabe cleared his throat. "Last Christmas was hard. Dad loved Christmas, and without him . . ." He swallowed. "It was rough."

"Same," Brittany said. "I cried a lot last December. And it was stressful. Mom always did the shopping, and the baking, all the little things that made Christmas special. I felt like I had to hold everything together for my brother and sister to make sure they didn't have this sad, miserable Christmas, but all I wanted to do was stay in bed."

I tugged at the seat belt pressing into my chest. "But . . . your parents *died*," I blurted out, feeling like a jerk for stating the obvious. "My dad's not gone, he's just in jail."

"You're still allowed to grieve, Brian," Mrs. Clelland said. "It's OK if the holidays feel hard. Be kind to yourself, all right? If you want to talk about anything, you know we're here."

Everything they were saying tilted me off balance. *I'm just having a bad day,* I wanted to insist, but it hit me how irritated I'd been by the decorations everywhere and cheesy music playing in every store and classmates talking about their plans for the break.

I thought about how Dad always lit up watching Richie tear into his gifts, and how we stayed up on Christmas night watching NBA games until I fell asleep on the couch.

I tried to stop, but it was too late. Tears started streaming down my face. Gabe slid into the middle seat and hugged me. When we reached my house, Mrs. Clelland parked and we sat there until I calmed down. Gabe kept an arm around me, and Brittany and Mrs. Clelland said comforting things.

I wasn't embarrassed about crying in front of them. They'd all seen me cry before. Usually, I felt better after I let it out and they gave me hugs and pep talks. But not today.

I said goodbye and hurried inside, where I headed for the shower and stayed in the steaming hot water until Richie banged on the door and asked if I was ever coming out.

By then, the bees in my chest had settled into a cold, hard brick.

10. VOLCANO

EZRA

The last week before the holiday break felt three months long. Everyone was hyper—except Brian, who'd gone quiet since the basketball game. I wanted to ask if he was OK, but he'd made it clear he didn't like that question, and I didn't know how to bring it up without making him feel worse.

And I kept seeing Victor and Colby everywhere, which felt awkward after my dream. I noticed Victor watching as Madi and I put up flyers around the school for the talent show. And I noticed Madi trying to melt his head every time she saw him.

I tried not to get caught up in drama, but I was curious enough to ask Madi about it while we were drinking hot chocolate at the mall after we went Christmas shopping.

She frowned. "Victor and Colby are jerks."

That was the short version. The long version had more twists than one of those true crime podcasts my mom loved.

Here was the medium version: Victor had spent the summer at his grandparents' house and ghosted Alicia. No texts, no calls, nothing. Colby and Jemma were already falling apart by mid-July ("Colby's so full of himself some-times," Madi complained, which, true), and Jemma dumped him after he kept defending Victor.

"The whole thing just made me realize that dating in junior high is silly," Madi said. "Most boys are so imma-ture. Except you, of course."

I didn't mention how often I made butt jokes with my friends. Instead, I raised my hot chocolate. "Thank you for recognizing that I'm a unicorn. But here's the more import-ant question: best Christmas song?"

"Easy," Madi said. "'All I Want for Christmas is You.'"

I shrugged. "Solid choice. But I'm going with 'This Christmas' by Donny Hathaway. It's from the seventies and is still a bop."

Madi wrinkled her nose. "I don't know it."

"We must fix that immediately. Here." I gave her an earbud and introduced her to great music, which was one of my purposes in life.

Finally, we got to break. The best part was Nat came to visit for a week. When Dad and I picked her up at the airport, she squealed and nearly tackled me in the arrivals area.

"Look at you! You're so tall! Is that a *mustache*?" She poked at the almost-invisible line of hair on my lip.

I pushed her hand away and grinned. "Good to see you, Nat."

It was great having her home. On Christmas Day, after we opened presents and ate a big breakfast, we video called our oldest sister, Lila, who was in Ontario with her mom and her husband and their four-month-old baby, Grace. Mostly we made silly faces at Grace. She was very cute.

The next day, Nat and I had our Boxing Day movie marathon. We'd done it every second year, when she spent Christmas with us. I'd invited Brian, Ty, and Kevan over too. I was glad Brian agreed to come and was both nervous and excited for Nat to meet him.

Kevan and Brian showed up together, and I led them to the basement and introduced them to Nat.

Brian waved. "Hey."

Nat smiled. "Nice to meet you! I've heard lots about you both."

"You too," Kevan said. "It sounds like you get all the credit for Ezra being so cool."

Nat laughed. "Absolutely."

I rolled my eyes. "All right, enough. Time to begin our formal program. Ty's coming later, so we can start without him." I swept my arm toward the TV. "Our first selection is *Sing Street*, about a budding young musician who learns to follow his dreams."

"Gee, I wonder why you picked this one," Kevan joked.

"Shut it, Kev." I scooped up a piece of caramel corn from the bowl on the coffee table and tossed it at his head. "You'll laugh, you'll cry, you'll feel inspiration stirring in your soul. So let's begin."

I loved *Sing Street*. I'd seen it three times already, so I watched my friends as much as I watched the movie. Kevan was clearly into it, but Brian was so quiet. I knew he'd visited his dad in jail yesterday, and I imagined that would be a hard way to spend Christmas. But maybe it was a sensitive subject. He didn't look like he wanted to talk. He didn't touch the snacks, either.

Ty showed up just as the movie ended.

"Sorry I'm late. Dad's family always gets together on Boxing Day, and I had to make an appearance." He plopped on the couch. "It's classic. Uncle Weldon asks how basketball is going, then he tells the same three stories from when he was in high school last century and lectures me about how players were tougher back then. Then when I offer to play him one-on-one, he mumbles about his bad knee, and my cousins crack up. I love it."

Kevan scooped up more caramel corn. "Roasting uncles is the best holiday tradition. I've been ragging on my uncle about his ratty high-waisted jeans since I was little. I think he wears the same pair every year just to bug me."

We riffed on more weird-uncle stories. Brian just sat there, and I remembered he didn't have much extended family—not that he ever saw, anyway. I wondered if we were making him feel worse, so I changed the subject.

"So . . . goofy comedy or pure action? Those are our choices." I looked at Brian. "You can pick. Or we could go with something else if you want."

He froze. "Uh . . . whatever. Comedy, I guess."

"Comedy it is." I loaded it up, and we laughed all the way through—except for Brian.

After it was over, Ty turned to him. "You're quiet, B. You all right?"

Brian looked pale. He swallowed. "I'm super tired. I might be getting sick, actually. I should probably go home."

The room went quiet. Brian looked so bummed. I wished I could make him feel better.

"You could chill in my room, if you want," I said.

"I don't want to give you my germs." He slowly stood up.

"Do you want a ride home?" Nat asked.

"No thanks. Maybe fresh air will help. Bye, everyone." He hurried for the stairs. I started to follow, then I remembered something in my room. I caught up just as he was pulling on his coat.

"I almost forgot, I got you a present." I handed him a gift bag. "Merry Christmas."

Brian blinked. "I . . . I didn't get you anything. I wanted to, but . . ."

He suddenly looked like he might cry.

"That's OK!" I said. "Honestly. It's nothing big. I just saw it and thought of you."

He opened the bag. I'd bought him a T-shirt with a dancing hot pepper saying "Spicy" in a cartoon speech bubble.

"This is . . ." Brian trailed off. "Thank you."

"Yeah, no problem. I hope you feel better soon. Text me when you get home."

I tried to sound casual, because Brian looked stressed. I hated that giving him a present made him think he was letting me down or something.

"OK. Bye." Then he left.

As we started another movie, I kept glancing at my phone. Brian sent one text. Home. Thanks again. I waited for him to say something else. I didn't know why.

We were all clearly distracted. It wasn't supposed to be like this.

When the credits rolled, I turned off the TV. "We have to help Brian. I think the holidays are making him sad."

"He does seem bummed," Ty agreed.

"No kidding," Kevan said. "He didn't eat any cookies. No healthy, happy person can resist my cookies."

I was glad they agreed with me. "We need a plan. Ty, maybe we should take him out to play ball. We can get some guys from the team and play three-on-three. Kevan, you could have him and Richie over to play video games."

By the time Kevan's dad picked him up, we had a schedule to check in with Brian all week. I said goodbye to my friends and then warmed up some apple cider in the microwave. When I turned around, Nat was leaning against the kitchen island, twirling a strand of hair.

"What?" I asked.

She hesitated. "It's sweet how you and your friends want to cheer Brian up."

There was a *but* coming. I could tell.

"But . . ." *There it is.* "He might not want to do all those things."

I rolled my eyes. "Oh, yeah. We're kidnapping him and forcing him to do stuff he likes. We're absolute monsters."

Nat only gave my joke a half-hearted smile. "Just don't get your hopes up. He didn't seem keen on being social today."

"He wasn't feeling well."

Nat twisted her hair. "Do you know if he's seeing anyone? Like a therapist, or . . . ?"

I dropped my mug down on the counter hard enough that cider sloshed out. "Jeez, Nat, it's not like I ask when's the last time he went to therapy. What are you getting at?"

"Well . . . he seems like he might be depressed."

"He spent Christmas visiting his dad in jail! Of course he's bummed out. That's why I'm trying to cheer him up."

"Ezra, that's the thing. Maybe he's more than bummed out." The louder I got, the softer Nat spoke, which made me more irritated. "You're a great friend. But if he's struggling with depression, that's not something you can fix. You can't put that kind of pressure on yourself."

For a second, I didn't know what to say. Then I said everything, like a volcano bubbled up inside of me.

"You don't know everything, Nat! You saw Brian for, like, three hours on a bad day. You don't know him at all. And you hardly know me anymore either."

Nat flinched. A voice in my head said *stop*, but it was no match for the volcano.

"You live a thousand miles away, and we talk online but that doesn't mean you know how I feel. Stop treating me like a little kid and mind your own business."

Nat stood there, just blinking. For once, she didn't have a quick comeback. I kind of wished she did. I didn't know what to do now. The thing about letting out a volcano was it left your insides scorched.

"I'm tired. I'm going to bed," I announced before Nat could say anything. I grabbed my mug and hurried to my room.

My electric guitar rested on my belly, unplugged, and I couldn't hear my muted chords as I strummed along to the song in my headphones. I trusted that my fingers were landing in the right places.

I'd never hear if Nat knocked on my door. I couldn't decide if I wanted her to burst in and try to fix whatever just happened, or if I wanted her to leave me alone. I wasn't used to being this mad at her.

I wished I could stop thinking about what she said.

"If he's struggling with depression . . ."

Brian would tell me if he was struggling, right? We tell each other stuff.

Except I was remembering the things I'd kept to myself lately, and the questions I hadn't asked. Maybe he did that with me too.

I set my guitar down and turned to the Internet to find

out how to tell if an eighth grader was depressed. The more I read, the worse I felt. Every line in the list of symptoms landed like a dart in my chest.

Loss of energy.

Changes in appetite.

Angry outbursts.

Social isolation.

I thought about the past few weeks. Brian was almost as silent as last year—except for his swear-fest in the middle of the game. He usually looked tired, and Kevan was right: He hadn't been eating. He left everything early. He didn't even want to be around us anymore.

Maybe he was just sick, like he said. Maybe he was sad about the holidays.

But what if it's more? What if Nat's right?

It took enormous willpower to wait until ten the next morning before I texted him.

Hey, hope you're feeling better. Want to go to the library?

The minutes stretched by in silence. He didn't write back until noon.

Sorry, still feeling like crap. Thanks though

I started a few replies, but I couldn't find the right words.

~~Is something bothering you~~

~~Want to talk~~

~~I could come over if~~

~~You'd tell me if you weren't OK, right?~~

Someone knocked on my door. "Are you decent?" Nat asked.

"Just finishing some nude yoga."

The joke came automatically, and Nat laughed. In that moment, I realized I wasn't mad anymore, and I was relieved she didn't seem mad either. Still, when I told her to come in, she closed the door and leaned against it, leaving most of the room and an awkward silence between us.

She took a breath. "Ezra—"

"I'm sorry," I blurted out. "I didn't mean—"

"No, it's OK." She bit her lip. "You were right."

"I was?"

She crossed the room and sat beside me. "I don't know Brian like you do. Maybe I jumped to conclusions. And . . . you're not the cute little sixth grader you were when I moved out." Nat forced a smile. "You're growing up. You're thoughtful and caring, and you've been doing fine without my advice. I miss you, that's all."

Her voice wobbled at the end. When I responded, I could only whisper.

"I miss you too, Nat."

She wrapped an arm around me, and I hugged her back. I was average height in my class, and I felt short next to Ty and Brian, but when Nat leaned against me, her head rested against my cheek.

"I'm proud of you, Ezra. Watching you with your friends . . . you're just *yourself*. It's great. Thanks for letting me hang out with you." She sighed. "But I have to get going."

"Aren't you leaving tomorrow?"

"I had to change my flight. There's a storm coming, and I have to work on the thirtieth. Dad's taking me to the airport in an hour."

"Oh."

My mind filled with all the things we hadn't talked about yet. I still wanted her advice on so many things, while she was *here*, not a face on my phone.

We went upstairs and ate lunch. Dad checked for airport-bound traffic updates on his tablet. When we said goodbye at the front door, Nat hugged me for a long time.

"I'm proud of you, Ezzy," she whispered. "Remember it's OK to think about what you want sometimes."

That was the second time she'd talked about what I *wanted*, and I wasn't sure what she meant, exactly. But I didn't get to ask, because she blew me one last kiss and slipped out the door.

11. JUST DO WHAT YOU CAN

BRIAN

New Year's Day is the most useless of all holidays. It's hard to feel excited about new beginnings when everything's frozen and gray. I spent most of the day in bed, moping about how bleak my whole holiday break had been.

No one should have to fake being happy on Christmas. But I'd tried, and so had Mom, for Richie's sake. He was smart enough to see through us, but he'd faked it too. He didn't complain when we took him to visit Dad.

I kind of wished he had. That would have felt more normal.

Dad had greeted us with a big phony smile and for an hour, we'd play-acted like a normal family. Richie barely said a word, which was how I knew he was miserable. But he'd held it together until we got home, then he burst into tears and ran to his room.

Ten-year-olds shouldn't cry on Christmas.

I wished I could have comforted him, but Mom and I had fallen apart too.

So that was Christmas. Sleep in heavenly peace or whatever.

My gloom had been a giant cloud at Ezra's Boxing Day movie marathon, until I couldn't take it anymore and bailed early. I felt awful for ruining one of Ezra's favorite days, especially when he'd gotten me a present and reminded me what a lousy friend I was.

He, Ty, and Kevan texted me every day, asking if I wanted to do something. I always sent the same reply. I'm not feeling great. Sorry. It wasn't a lie.

★★★

When school started back up on Tuesday, I showered, got dressed, and forced down a slice of toast. I reached the door and stared at my boots. That was when a picture of the day formed: the slow walk on frozen sidewalks, the noise as three hundred kids piled into the building, the hours droning by in classrooms that were too hot or too cold.

I couldn't do it.

I told Mom I felt sick, then I went back to my room. She tried talking to me, but I didn't come out. When she gave up, I heard Richie peppering her with questions—*What's wrong with Brian? How come he gets to stay home?*

I put my pillow over my head.

I tried again on Wednesday, but I started crying in the bathroom.

On Thursday I didn't get up at all.

Somehow, it was three P.M. when Mom came in and sat on my bed. I must have fallen asleep, or maybe I'd zoned out all day. It all felt the same.

I was supposed to be helping Mom and Richie, but I wasn't. I was making them worry. I was hurting them. I was wrecking all the progress I'd made. I'd even missed basketball practice, and Coach was probably going to bench me or kick me off the team.

I was failing. At everything. But I couldn't do anything about it. I was sinking into a hole.

"I made you a doctor's appointment," Mom said. "And an appointment with Dr. Bender. Both are next Tuesday."

That was less than a week away. The medical system never moved that fast. Not for most people, anyway. I pictured Mom pleading into the phone. Maybe she'd called our social worker for backup. I probably had a bright orange sticker on my file.

This kid's been in care. His mom's been in the psychiatric hos-pital. Diagnosis: disaster waiting to happen.

"You're in a rough patch, Brian. It happens. But we'll get it sorted out."

Mom tried to sound low-key, like my *rough patch* was a stomach bug or a sprained ankle. She spoke slowly, choosing words like they were jellybeans and she was trying to avoid one that tasted like a sock.

She leaned over and planted a kiss on my forehead. "This won't last forever. I promise."

★★★

An hour later, Richie plopped onto my bed, practically sitting on me.

"You have to get up tomorrow," he announced. "No more staying in bed."

I groaned and tried to roll away. He threw his weight across my chest. His face hovered over mine, so close our noses were almost touching.

"Tomorrow. You. Get. Up." His breath smelled like peanut butter. He jabbed a finger in my forehead with each word. "Promise. Me."

I wanted to toss him to the floor, but my arms were pinned under my blanket.

"Get off," I growled.

"Not until you promise."

"Richie—"

"Promise!"

Richie could be the most stubborn kid on earth. He got this look in his eye that meant *Give me what I want or it's going to get messy.* And right now, he wanted his brother out of bed.

No, he needed it.

Last June, when Dad left and Mom fell apart, all we had was each other. I couldn't crumble on Richie. I couldn't break down like our parents had. I couldn't do this to him. I couldn't.

"All right. I promise."

He didn't move. "You mean it?"

"Richie!" Mom came tearing in and yanked him off my bed. She marched him away, but my door was open, and I heard her low, urgent tones. Richie's voice rose in reply. Then he stormed to his room and slammed the door.

"I mean it," I said to no one. "I promise."

"Are you sure?" Mom asked again as I zipped up my parka on Friday morning. I wasn't sure at all, but I had to do this. For Richie, and for me.

She exhaled. "Just . . . do what you can manage. If you need to call me—"

"I'll be fine." I said it like I believed it.

Kevan walked to school with me. He talked like it was a normal day, which helped distract me. I made it to school without falling apart. Facing Ezra was harder, because I knew he was worried. But he and Ty both greeted me with a fist bump and a simple *hey*. They were playing it casual too. That was good.

I had PE first period, which meant I had to see Coach Williams. *Might as well get that over with too.* I approached him while my classmates were still in the locker room.

"Hey, Coach," I said. "Sorry I've been missing practice. I haven't been at school all week. I haven't been feeling well."

My stomach twisted as he looked me over. I was worried he'd be upset, or he'd ask questions, but he didn't. "That's OK, Brian. You can take it easy today. Just do what you can."

I swallowed. "Thanks, Coach."

I muddled through a half-speed game of badminton with Ezra. Moving helped my head feel a little clearer, and the break from my fog carried me through French. Third period was math. After we settled, Mrs. Woolaver started handing out a quiz.

My chest seized. When she reached my desk, I struggled to force out the words. "Mrs. Woolaver, I, um, I've been out sick. I'm behind."

"It's mostly review from before the holidays, Brian. Just do what you can." She handed me a test and moved on.

Mom and Coach Williams had both said the same thing. *Just do what you can.*

Ten minutes later, I'd only written my name. These questions might as well be in hieroglyphs.

This was a mistake.

Papers rustled as everyone turned to stare. Ezra was wide-eyed.

Apparently I'd said that out loud.

Mrs. Woolaver looked up. "No talking."

I dropped my pencil and put my head in my hands. "I can't do this."

Behind me, someone giggled. Ezra whirled in his seat. "Shut *up*," he snapped.

Mrs. Woolaver raised her voice. "People. Not another word."

I gathered my binder, which was hard because my hands were shaking. My pencil rolled onto the floor, and I left it there. My heart was racing and my eyes burned and there was a good chance I was about to burst into tears. There was no way I was letting that happen here.

I stood up.

So did Mrs. Woolaver. "Brian—"

"I can't do this." My voice shook and everyone was staring and I hated this, but I kept going because I needed to leave *right now*. "You said do what I can, and I can't do anything. I'm sorry."

Maybe she responded, but I couldn't tell because my ears started ringing as I bolted. Five steps down the hall, I realized I wasn't going to cry; I was having a supermassive panic attack. My heart raced, my lungs locked up, and my eyes went starry. Everything just . . . disappeared.

"Hey," a voice said. "Hey. Brian."

The fog cleared slowly. I was on my side. I felt cold tile against my cheek—and someone's hand on my shoulder.

It was Victor. This had to be a dream, because I'd been in math and now I was on the floor and Victor was here and he was calling me Brian. Not *Weirdo* or *Freak* or *Ghost*.

"You blacked out for a second," Victor said. "Don't move, OK? I'll go get—"

He didn't finish, because Ezra tackled him.

"What did you do?" Ezra shouted in Victor's face. His voice echoed down the hall. Classroom doors opened and teachers came running.

This wasn't a dream. Reality rushed in as the hall filled with noise. Ezra was angrier than I'd ever seen him. It took two teachers to pull him off Victor. Then the guidance counselor, Mrs. Barton, was beside me asking questions, and too many people were talking, and it was all so much.

Someone said *ambulance*. I sat up. My head swam and Mrs. Barton told me to take it easy, but I slowly pushed to my feet. I didn't want an ambulance. I didn't want strangers prodding me and asking more questions. I wasn't going to the hospital.

"I just want to go home," I croaked.

Mrs. Barton helped me to the office. I was still wobbly and I focused on putting one foot in front of the other, but I could tell people were watching. I made it to the sick room and lay down on a cot before my last bit of dignity crumbled and I broke down and cried.

12. SUCKAPALOOZA

EZRA

Victor and I sat in the principal's office, as far apart as the room allowed. We didn't speak until Ms. Floriman came in and closed the door. She sighed, like she was thinking, *Right, after everything else, I have to deal with you two.*

She sat at her desk. "Tell me what happened. Victor, you first."

Victor stretched. "I came out of the bathroom and saw Brian in the hall. He looked like he was going to be sick, then he started to fall over. I caught him and put him on his side so he didn't hurt himself. I was about to get help when Ezra tackled me."

"You *caught* him?" I blurted out. "Sure. You're Spider-Man."

"Ezra," Ms. Floriman scolded.

I felt like I'd swallowed hot coals. I'd never been in a fight before. I'd never yelled at a teacher until I argued with Mrs. Woolaver and stormed out to find Brian. I hated everything about today.

"Is there anything else you want to tell me?" Ms. Floriman asked Victor.

"Nope." He looked at me. "Your turn."

Victor was so calm, and I felt the opposite. I pinched the skin between my thumb and index finger.

"Brian was on the ground, with Victor hovering over him. I thought Victor was going to kick him. So I tackled Victor before he could hurt him."

"I was kneeling," Victor said. "You can't kick someone when you're kneeling."

"Victor—"

"You could have punched him or choked him!"

"*Boys.*" Ms. Floriman held up her hands. "Ezra, did you see Victor hurt Brian?"

My knee bounced. "No, but Victor hates Brian. Do you honestly think he was trying to help?"

Ms. Floriman turned to Victor. "You two do have a history."

"The history where Brian broke my nose?" Victor asked.

I couldn't help laughing. "Are you serious? You bullied him! You made him miserable all year and you're still sitting there all quiet and smug about it, like a psychopath."

Ms. Floriman gasped. Victor turned pink, then red. He clenched his fists so hard I thought his knuckles might burst through his skin.

"Victor," Ms. Floriman said slowly, in the tone

scientists used in monster movies when they were trying not to set off the giant murder lizard.

I'd gone too far. But before I could take it back, Victor closed his eyes and drew a deep breath. The color drained from his cheeks as he exhaled in a long, steady *hooooo*.

"I know I was mean last year," he said slowly. "But I never beat anyone up. I don't do that. And this year, I haven't bothered Brian, or anyone else, at all. I get why you don't believe me, but I'm telling the truth: I was just trying to help."

His voice was even again, like those ten seconds when he looked ready to blow had never happened. I couldn't decide if that was impressive or scary. But I had a nagging feeling that he was telling the truth. I knew Brian wasn't doing well, and he'd looked awful when he rushed out of math. Whatever happened in the hall, there was a good chance Victor didn't cause it.

I squirmed. I didn't want to be here. I needed to find Brian and see if he was OK.

The bell rang. Ms. Floriman glanced at the clock.

"All right, here's what I'm thinking. Victor, I don't have any reason to doubt you. And Ezra, your reaction was a bit much, but I understand why your emotions were running high. And you're not hurt, are you, Victor?"

He shrugged. "I'm fine."

Mrs. Floriman paused. "If you need a minute, or if you'd like to talk to—"

"I'm fine," Victor repeated.

The principal sighed. "Well, how about you apologize, Ezra, and we put this behind us? And in the future, please find a staff member instead of taking matters into your own hands. Now you should both head to your next class."

We stood. Heat filled my face.

"Sorry," I grunted. Ms. Floriman sighed but didn't say anything.

"OK." Victor tucked his hands in his pockets. "I don't hate him," he said as he passed me. He left without waiting for a reply.

I had a bunch of questions about what had just happened, but none of that mattered right now.

"Can I see Brian?" I asked Ms. Floriman.

Her face softened. "Mrs. Barton is with him. I know you two are close, but you should let him rest."

"Oh. OK." I turned to leave.

"Ezra," Ms. Floriman said, "maybe you should talk to Mrs. Barton later too. For your own benefit."

Talk to the guidance counselor? "I'm fine, Ms. Floriman. I'm just worried about Brian. I won't start tackling people in the hall every day. Promise."

She smiled. "I know. But being worried about a friend is not a small thing. If you ever want some support, we're here."

I paused. The way she said it made me think about how Nat kept asking what I wanted.

"Thanks," I said. "I'll think about it."

Brian didn't answer my text. I checked with Kevan and Ty, and he hadn't texted them either, so I tried not to take it personally. But I couldn't just sit around and do nothing. One thing I *wanted* was to make sure my best friend was OK. So after practice, I walked to Brian's house.

Mrs. Clelland's car was in the driveway. When I knocked on the door, Brian's mom looked surprised to see me. Her eyes were red, like she was tired, or she'd been crying. Or both.

"I brought my notes from this week," I said. "I thought Brian might want them later. Can I talk to him?"

She hesitated before opening the door. "He's in his room. I don't think he's in the mood for company. But come in."

Mrs. Clelland and Gabe were at the kitchen table. The moms were drinking tea and Gabe had a half-empty glass of water. It was clear they'd been talking before I showed up. I felt out of place, the kid among two adults and an almost-adult. But Gabe gave me a fist bump, and Mrs. Clelland smiled as I sat down. We were all here, and being here made me feel a little better.

Brian's door creaked open, and he shuffled to the kitchen. He was barefoot in shorts and a bathrobe. He glanced around the table and froze.

"Hey," his mom said gently. "Are you hungry? I can heat you up some soup."

Brian shook his head. Then he turned and went back to his room.

His mom's shoulders deflated. Mrs. Clelland and Gabe gave each other a *what do we do now?* look.

I hopped up and hurried after him.

"Ezra, I don't know . . ." Mrs. Clelland started, but no one stopped me.

The sun was setting and Brian's room was dim. The only light came from his bedside lamp. He was lying on his bed with a book.

"I thought I'd spend the night," I said. "If that's OK with you."

Brian looked up. "Was this Mom's idea?"

"I haven't asked her yet. I wanted to ask you first. We don't have to talk or anything. We can watch the Raptors game, or whatever you want."

He hung his head. "I don't know. I'm like the least fun person alive right now. You should just see if Kevan wants to instead."

I took a step closer to the bed. "Brian. You're my best friend. Nothing's going to change that." I swallowed. "Do you think, um, maybe you're depressed?"

Brian blinked a lot. I moved closer.

"If you are, it's OK to say it. You don't need to pretend you've got the flu or whatever. We're the Weirdo Alliance. We're supposed to tell each other stuff."

After a long silence, Brian sat up. "I don't know.

Maybe. Probably." He wiped his eyes. "You know, you're a lot sometimes."

"I wrestled Victor to the floor for you, so yeah, I am. Deal with it."

Brian snorted. It was the closest to a laugh I'd heard from him in two weeks.

I sat next to him. "I didn't need to tackle Victor, did I?"

He sighed. "No, he was actually trying to help. I'm so pathetic that even Victor feels too sorry for me to pick on me anymore."

I nudged him with my elbow. "Listen. You're allowed to say one miserable thing like that per hour. Any more and I'm going to sing all the worst Maroon 5 songs at you."

Brian side-eyed me. "I don't agree to those terms."

"They're nonnegotiable. Sorry, not sorry."

He rolled his eyes. I grinned. I guess this meant he was OK with me staying.

But now I was thinking about Victor. I'd jumped him, accused him of something he didn't do, and called him a psychopath in front of the principal. He could have lost it on me, but he held back. When I had him pinned to the floor, he didn't fight. He didn't even yell at me to get off. He didn't do anything.

"I think . . . maybe Victor's changed," I said. "He seems different."

Brian stared at me. "Different how?" I wasn't sure if it was a question or an accusation, like *How dare you say nice things about the guy who bullied me.*

Before I could answer, Gabe knocked and stepped into the room. "The moms sent me as their delegate to make sure everything's all right."

"We're fine," Brian said. "Tell Mom that Ezra's spending the night."

"Tell her yourself," Gabe replied. "Stop being a hermit for a few minutes."

Brian flopped back on his bed. "Ugh. You guys are the worst."

"I hear you," Gabe said. "But I know what you mean is, 'I love you, Gabe and Ezra, and I know you love me, and thanks for not letting me wallow here all alone in mopey town.'"

I grinned. "'All Alone in Mopey Town' is a perfect title for a country song." I put on a twangy drawl. "*I'm all alone in mopey town / Got the blues, feelin' down—*"

Brian made a noise somewhere between a laugh and a strangled scream. "Fine. But we're not talking about what happened at school. And I'm not getting dressed."

Gabe poked Brian's belly. "Deal. Now come on."

We had a not-terrible night. Gabe stayed for a while, and Richie came home from Leo and Kevan's house after supper. We watched the Raptors play the Houston Rockets, and Richie and Gabe joked around and booed James Harden, the Rockets' bearded scoring machine. Brian curled under a blanket and didn't say much. He didn't eat any of the popcorn his mom made, and he burrowed deeper without answering when she asked if he wanted anything else. But he was here, at least, and not alone in his room.

When we were settled in the dark at bedtime, me on the floor in a sleeping bag, I thought about bringing up Victor again. But maybe it was too much to ask Brian about right now. I wasn't sure what to talk about. None of my questions seemed right to ask. We settled into a heavy silence.

I fell asleep eventually, and I woke when the floor-board squeaked beside my head. It was still dark. Brian was a fuzzy blob perched on the edge of his bed. I fumbled for my glasses and slid them onto my face.

"Sorry," Brian said. "I didn't mean to wake you."

I checked my phone. It was almost three A.M. "Have you been awake all night?"

He shrugged. "Most of it. Nights are crappy again."

That was the most he'd willingly told me in a while. I sat up and shivered. Brian's room was cold. I pulled the sleeping bag up around my chest.

"What's going on in your head right now?" I asked.

"You don't want to know."

"Yes, I do."

Brian slid to the far edge of his bed, against the wall. I climbed out of the sleeping bag and lay down beside him. He stared at the ceiling.

"Everything just . . . sucks. I don't know how else to describe it. I'm swirling around in a giant toilet bowl of suck."

"Suckorama," I said.

Brian yawned. "Suckmageddon."

"Suckapalooza."

"A suckstorm of infinite suckage."

We went quiet.

"You don't, um . . ." I took a shaky breath. It felt like a horrible thing to ask, but I had to say it. "You don't feel like dying or anything, do you?"

Brian's pause lasted forever.

Then he swallowed hard. "The day Mom took all her pills was the worst day of my life. I hate everything right now, but I could never make Richie go through another day like that."

"Uh, good." My throat was scratchy. "But it's not just Richie, OK? I love you. And so does Gabe, and Brittany, and Kevan, and Ty, and lots of people. So promise me you'll tell us if things get really bad. You don't have to tell me, if you don't want. Just tell somebody."

Brian sighed. "OK. If you promise . . ."

He trailed off. I rolled toward him.

"Promise what?"

"I keep thinking you'll leave," he said in a tiny voice. "Because it's too hard to be my friend."

"Brian. Never. I promise."

I asked if it was OK to hug him, and he said yes. He felt so skinny and cold in my arms, like he was fading. I held on to him for as long as he let me.

It was light out when I woke again. Brian was asleep. I carefully got up, pulled on a hoodie, and slipped out of the room. The Days' house was quiet except for the click of buttons on a controller. Richie was on the couch, playing a Star Wars game. I sat beside him.

"Brian's still in bed?"

"Yeah."

Riche's chin twitched. "He's always in his bed."

"It's tough, huh?"

"I'm not supposed to be mad at him. Mom says it's not his fault." Richie kept his eyes on his game, but his eyebrows furrowed.

"I miss him too, Richie." I slid closer. "Want a player two?"

"Sure."

I picked up a controller. "Hey, which do you think is a better band name?" I asked as we brought down an AT-AT walker. "Pizza Wizard, or Homemade Ghosts? I also like The Biracial Unicorn Experience, but that might be too long. It needs to look good on a T-shirt, you know?"

Richie glanced at me. "They're all weird."

"Weird is my *brand*, Rich. Hey, can you play bass? My band could use a bass player."

Richie shook his head. "Do you even have a band?"

"Not yet. So this is your opportunity. You don't want to look back when you're old and think, *I could have been in the Rock and Roll Hall of Fame.* So, what do you say? Can you learn the bass by, like, Thursday?"

Richie giggled. "You *are* weird."

"Thank you."

Brian stayed in bed a long time, but Richie and I spent an hour blowing up the Empire, and it wasn't a bad way to start the morning.

13. CATEGORY FIVE BRAIN SHARKNADO

BRIAN

My doctors' appointments on Tuesday gave me an excuse to skip school again. I stayed home on Monday too. Mom couldn't argue after my legendary disaster on Friday.

I wasn't sure I could ever go back. A guy could only suffer so many embarrassments in junior high, and I'd had my share already.

The worst part of the day was leaving the house. I hadn't done that since Friday. I hadn't even visited Dad on Sunday. It was one more thing I felt awful about, but visiting jail would have been even harder than going to school.

I suggested to Mom that maybe Dr. Bender could do a video chat, but that didn't fly.

"You are going outside," Mom said.

So I dressed and forced down half the smoothie Mom made me for breakfast. It had blueberries and spinach and protein powder and some weird seeds. It tasted like sand—everything tasted like sand—and the seeds got stuck in my teeth. But I drank some because Mom wouldn't leave me alone otherwise. She was constantly trying to feed me now. It was annoying.

I tried to convince her that if I had to go out, she should let me go alone, but that didn't fly either. She'd taken the day off work. I was stuck with her. When we got on the bus, I sat a row away and stuck in my earbuds. My chest fluttered and I couldn't stop my fingers from trembling, but I didn't have another panic attack, so that was something.

I felt better once I was past the waiting room and sitting on the comfy green sofa in Dr. Bender's office. I didn't mind it there, actually. I'd dreaded starting therapy back in the summer, because *hello*, social anxiety. A fifty-minute personal conversation with a stranger sounded as fun as swimming naked in a piranha tank. But Dr. Bender had quickly set me at ease.

"Good morning, Brian," she said today. "Want the usual?"

I nodded, and she brought me a mug of hot water and a lemon-ginger tea bag. We'd figured out that holding a warm mug helped me relax. As the tea steeped, I glanced at the watercolor painting of Aang from *Avatar: The Last Airbender* above Dr. Bender's desk. A high school patient of hers painted it, she'd told me in my first session. It was a play on her last name. She'd said if she could be a real bender, she'd choose airbending, like Aang.

"Coasting around on a swirling ball of air seems pretty neat to me," she'd said. *"What kind of bender would you be?"*

I'd told her I'd have to think about it. In our second session I picked a waterbender, since I loved the ocean. Talking got easier from there.

She sat across from me. "So. What's happening?"

I started telling her everything I couldn't tell Ezra in the middle of the night, and once I started, everything came pouring out in a giant word-barf. "Basically, everything's terrible. I feel awful, all the time. Eating feels like work. I'm always tired, but I can't sleep. I hate being alone with my garbage brain, but trying to be around people is too hard. I don't want to read, I have no energy to play ball, I don't want to do anything. I'm letting everyone down and screwing up my whole life, but I can't do anything to stop it."

Dr. Bender nodded. "And are you having any suicidal thoughts?"

I shook my head. "No. I'm just . . . scared, I guess."

She leaned forward. "Can you tell me why?"

I glanced at Aang, balanced happily on his ball of air. "It just doesn't make sense. I know why I was having panic attacks when I first saw you. But things are better now. Mom's OK, most of the time. I have friends. I'm doing well in school and basketball—well, I was, anyway." I sipped my tea. "I shouldn't be depressed, right? Nothing bad was happening. My brain's just broken. So I guess I'm scared I won't get better this time."

"That's an understandable fear."

I liked that Dr. Bender never said anything useless like "It's going to be OK." She never seemed surprised by my weird and ugly thoughts either. Her general vibe was *Your issues are real, but I've seen worse*. It was kind of comforting.

She reached for her tea. "It does sound like you're dealing with depression, Brian. Any number of things could have brought it on. Hormones, for starters. You must be five or six inches taller than when I met you. A growth spurt like that does all kinds of things with your body chemistry. Puberty is a heck of a time."

"No kidding," I muttered. Dr. Bender smiled.

"It sounds like you noticed a change in early December," she continued. "Lots of people have a hard time around the holidays, or over the winter when it's cold and dark. That doesn't mean you'll feel this way every year, but the season could be a factor. Even positive changes, like new friendships or a bigger role with the basketball team, can introduce new stresses. And you went through a major trauma barely six months ago. Healing doesn't happen quickly, or in a straight line. It's natural to have ups and downs. Any or all of those factors could be affecting you."

"Like a perfect storm," I said. "A category five sharknado in my brain."

"That's one way to put it."

"Great. So how do I beat a brain sharknado?"

"That's the million-dollar question," Dr. Bender said. "The good news is you've built up some resiliency over the past six months. You have a good support network. Try to stay connected with the people who care about you, even when you don't feel like it. Keep up with the healthy eating and exercise. Try to get regular sleep." She read the expression on my face. "That one's not easy, I take it."

"Nope."

Dr. Bender paused for a moment. "When you see your family doctor, I'd suggest that you discuss whether medication might be a good option for you."

"Oh." I picked at a loose thread on the cuff of my hoodie.

"How do you feel about that?"

"Not great."

"Can you tell me why?"

She waited while I thought. I also liked that Dr. Bender didn't mind silence. When you struggled to say things out loud like I did, sometimes people filled the gaps by asking more questions or trying to guess what I was thinking. They threw more information at my SAWS-addled brain while I was still trying to respond to the first thing they'd said, and I got overloaded and shut down.

Dr. Bender didn't do that. She gave me time to breathe.

"It's going to sound terrible," I said.

"You know everything is fair game here."

I swallowed. "I'm afraid of being like my mom."

Dr. Bender nodded, as if to say, *I hear you. Go on.* So I did. I said all the worst things. Mom had been on medication as long as I could remember, and sometimes it seemed to work and sometimes it didn't. Then one day she'd taken a bunch at once and my life fell apart.

Finally, I said the ugliest thing of all.

"Sometimes I feel like this is her fault. Like maybe she gave me the genes that made my brain like this. And then she did the thing that really broke me. Well, I guess that was Dad's fault too." I looked up. "I know it's not very original to blame everything on my parents, but I can't stop thinking about it."

Dr. Bender didn't even flinch, didn't say *What a horrible thought, you rotten brat.* She sipped her tea. "Would it be fair to say your parents are flawed people who still love you very much?"

"Sounds about right."

"So, the question is, what do you do about that?"

"Huh?"

"Well, some kids run away and join the circus."

I let out a *heh*. "Are circuses even a thing anymore? Besides, I tried running away when we were in foster care. Richie got grumpy when we ran out of food."

"Fair enough. Having to feed yourself all the time is overrated. That's a clear strike against running away."

One more point for Dr. Bender: Sometimes her jokes were as dark and weird as mine.

"The other option is to keep working through your complicated feelings," she said. "Like you're doing right now. And use whatever tools are most helpful. Maybe medication will be one of those things, and maybe it won't. It's not a magic cure. Some people find medication helps for a season. Some are on it for longer. But I'd encourage you to talk it over with your doctor."

In our last few minutes, she reminded me about everything I was doing well at, and she booked me another appointment for the next week. I left her office feeling better, but I was still lost in thought about medication. I didn't notice the other kid in the waiting room until he said, "Oh."

It was Victor.

I was so surprised I just stood there, staring.

"Awkward, right?" Victor said.

He smirked, but it wasn't mean. I knew Victor's mean smirk by heart. This was different.

"Uh . . . yeah," I choked out.

We were spared from saying anything else when a man with tortoiseshell glasses stepped out from an office behind me and waved at Victor. "Come on in."

Victor got up. He nodded as he passed me. "See you, Brian."

"Was that someone from school?" Mom asked as we made our way to the elevators.

"Yeah." I didn't say any more. She knew how Victor had treated me last year, but she'd never met him. And I didn't want to revisit all that right now.

I couldn't help wondering, though. Victor had used my name again. He wasn't picking on me anymore. And he was going to therapy. Ezra had said he seemed different. Had he really changed?

Whatever. I didn't have enough energy to waste thinking more about Victor.

My family doctor's office wasn't as chill as Dr. Bender's. The waiting room was full. Whiny kids, stressed moms, and one older man who kept glaring like we'd all invaded his living room. I stuck in my earbuds and closed my eyes until Mom tapped my arm.

She came in with me. I could have argued that I wanted to go in alone, but I just wanted to get it over with. Dr. Murphy weighed me, measured me, listened to my heart, and checked my blood pressure. We went over the same questions everyone kept asking. Eventually we left with a reminder card for a follow-up next week and a yellow prescription slip for antidepressants.

"I think this is for the best, Brian," Mom said as we headed for the bus. I stuck in my earbuds.

Mom got off the bus near the pharmacy, but I rode straight home to go back to bed. Later in the afternoon, Mom called me into the kitchen. There was a blue pill bottle on the counter.

She handed me the leaflet from the pharmacy. "In case you want to read the fine print. I think we should keep these in the kitchen, on the shelf above the fridge."

I shook off a vivid memory of finding two bottles on Mom's bedroom floor, empty.

She kept her pills on the shelf above the fridge now too.

After I took my first green-and-white pill, I snapped a picture of the bottle and sent it to our group chat.

Me: Guess who's on drugs

Ty: Congratulations

Ezra: That's good right? They're supposed to help?

Me: That's the point, yeah

Me: Sorry that was sarcastic

Ezra: I forgive you dingus

Kevan: Do they have cool side effects? Like night vision or chest hair?

Ezra: Kevan jeez

Me: Apparently they might cause stomach problems. Like my stomach's not messed enough already

Kevan: No kidding dude you poop all the time

Ty: No poop shaming, Kevan

Kevan: I take it back. Poop as much as you need B

Me: The official warning says I may also experience diminished interest in sex

Kevan: lololol

Everyone made more jokes after that. I realized I'd missed this, everybody piling on and being ridiculous. I guess Dr. Bender was right about staying connected.

I sent Ezra a side text. I told Dr. Bender everything. What you said the other night kind of helped. So thanks.

He texted back a heart and a fist-bump emoji.

I was feeling almost decent—almost—when Mom came into my room.

"How do you feel about school tomorrow?" she asked.

I didn't look up from my phone. "I feel that would be a bad idea."

"Can we talk about why?"

"What's there to talk about? Last time was a disaster. So I'm done."

Mom's voice tightened. "What do you mean, *done*?"

"I mean I'll do school at home."

"Brian, you're not dropping out of junior high."

"It's not dropping out. Lots of kids homeschool. I looked it up. I'll send you a link."

"Look—can you put your phone down? Please?"

The *please* made me angry. It was like she was afraid to upset me, like she was worried I'd break.

"I know this is hard," she said. "Trust me, I know."

"No you don't," I said. "You know what it's like for you. I'm not you."

Mom blinked. "I know that too. You're stronger than me, Brian. You've been through so much already, and you've never stopped trying. But I need you to keep trying, honey."

"Great pep talk."

Mom sighed. "I get it. You don't want to talk to me about any of this. That's fair. Maybe you think it's my fault."

I didn't answer. Mom looked so hurt that normally I would have felt awful. But I didn't. It was like one more part of me that wasn't working right.

Mom pressed on. "You've come so far, Brian. I know that's hard to see right now, but you have. So keep trying,

OK? Talk to Dr. Bender, talk to Gabe, talk to Jackie Clelland, talk to Ezra. Just keep trying."

Mom reached out to touch my shoulder. I went stiff, and her hand hovered for a moment. Then, with another sigh, she left me alone.

14. BOHEMIAN RHAPSODY, PART II

EZRA

As I got ready for school, I checked our group text. There wasn't anything new since our conversation last night. I read it again.

> **Kevan:** So are you coming back to school now?
> **Brian:** I don't know. Not tomorrow
> **Me:** I'll pick up homework and stuff for you
> **Ty:** Let us know when you're ready B. We got your back

I kept glancing at my phone, hoping for a last-minute update: Changed my mind. See you at school. But it didn't come. I wondered if I should text him some encouragement. He'd said it had helped when I'd nudged him to talk at the sleepover. But I didn't want to be pushy or annoying, and I didn't know what to say, so I didn't say anything.

When I stepped inside Halifax North, I wiped steam off my glasses from the change in temperature and tried to stop thinking about Brian. Right now, I had to find Victor.

It wasn't something I wanted to do, but I felt bad about what I'd said to him. I'd looked for him on Monday, but he'd been with Colby whenever I saw him, and yesterday I hadn't seen him at all.

As I passed the music room, I heard the piano. I peeked in and spotted the back of Victor's head. I crossed the room, trying to be loud enough that I didn't startle him. He finally looked up and stopped playing.

"That's the beginning of 'Bohemian Rhapsody,'" I said.

He gave his tiny smile. "It's fun to play."

"It sounds great. Are you doing it for the talent show?"

"I haven't decided what to play yet. You?"

"Same. Do you come here a lot before school?"

"Sometimes."

Suddenly I had questions. *How long have you been playing piano? What bands do you like?* But between his short answers and raised eyebrows, I figured he wanted me to get to the point and leave him alone.

I let it out in a rush. "I need to apologize for Friday. For real this time. Brian told me you really were trying to help. So, I'm sorry I tackled you, I'm sorry I didn't believe you, and I'm *really* sorry I called you a psychopath. That was gross. I told Ms. Floriman all this too, so she knows it wasn't your fault. Sorry."

Victor's face wavered for a second before it was back to stone. "Apology accepted."

That's it? I didn't know what I was expecting. But Victor was just . . . inscrutable. That was the word.

I blew out a breath. "Should we shake on it or something?"

"Sure." He stuck out his hand, and I shook it. Victor had long fingers, perfect for playing piano. And his grip was strong. He watched me with his head tilted as we shook hands, and my cheeks suddenly grew warm.

"Uh, I'll let you go back to playing now." I started for the door.

"There's something you could do to make it up to me."

I paused. "You accepted my apology. I don't owe you a debt or anything."

"True, but I could use a guitar player."

"What?"

"I'm working on this instrumental. I think it could use some guitar." Victor pulled out his phone. "I can play you what I've got so far."

Of course I was curious about what kind of music Victor was making. He set his phone on the ledge of the piano. As the music played, he sat perfectly still. I wished I had a clue what he was thinking. If I was playing him something I'd recorded, I'd be nervous as heck.

His song started with simple repeating piano chords. A sparse beat and bass line came in next, then an airy synthesizer. A tinkling melody wandered in and out. The piece had a lo-fi electronic vibe but there was a hint of tension too. It made me think of sitting on the porch of an old house as the wind picked up and rustled the wind chimes.

Victor hit pause. "You get the idea. It loops like that and then fades out."

"That's cool," I said. "You did all that on a computer?"

He nodded. "It needs something, though. I'm thinking a guitar might beef it up. Nothing complicated, just—"

"I know what you mean." I already could hear an idea, filling the spaces where the melody dropped out. "Not too much. I like how it sounds so open. Some swells might sound good."

"Yeah, that might work. I can send it to you, if you want. If you come up with anything I could bring my laptop over and we could record."

I nodded and gave Victor my number before the homeroom bell rang. He sent me a link to his song at lunch. I saw the notification while I was eating with Kevan and Ty, and a flash of heat passed through me.

"Is that Brian?" Ty asked, and I felt horrible.

I shook my head. "I should check in with him, though." I texted Brian, so I didn't have to talk about who was actually texting me.

Me: How are you? Want me to come over after school?

He wrote back just before the end of lunch.

Brian: I'm OK. Gabe's picking me up later
Mom says if I don't leave my room she'll read love
scenes from romance novels out loud until I melt
from embarrassment. She's a monster
Anyway, you can come if you want but no
pressure

This was more than he'd written in a while. That was a good sign, maybe? And he was hanging out with Gabe, so he was in good hands.

I wrote back, you guys go ahead, talk to you tonight

I didn't tell him that I couldn't wait to work on music for Victor, but it was true. Ideas were bubbling up and I couldn't wait to get home and pick up my guitar.

After school I headed to my room and looped his song on my phone while I tried out different riffs. I played around with my reverb and delay pedals to change the tone. I made up my own bits of music sometimes, and I'd learned lots of covers, but experimenting over Victor's loop was a new kind of thrill. It was like he'd handed me a cake and I could decorate it however I wanted. Chocolate or vanilla icing, sprinkles, M&M'S . . .

Mom knocked. "Ezra? Dinner's ready. You didn't hear me calling?"

I hit stop and noticed the time. I hadn't left my room in two hours.

Mom looked at my guitar slung over my shoulder and smiled. "In the groove, huh? Well, take a break and come eat."

After dinner, I texted Victor. Thanks for sending me your track. I came up with some stuff I like if you want to hear it sometime

He wrote back a few minutes later. Cool. I could bring my laptop over tomorrow if you want. Or tonight if you're not busy

Me: Tonight?
Victor: Why not?

I checked with Mom, then I wrote back. Sure, you could come tonight. Then I gave him my address. My belly fluttered as I hit send.

15. KEEP SHOOTING

BRIAN

My knee bounced as I sat in the passenger seat of the Clellands' car. Gabe still hadn't told me where we were going. When he picked me up, he only told me to get ready to play ball. I told him I couldn't handle going to a public gym or being around a lot of people.

"Trust me, I got this," he replied.

I did trust him, but my chest buzzed when he pulled into the school parking lot.

"Trust me," he repeated before I could ask why he'd brought me to a place I'd been avoiding. He parked, sent a quick text, and led me to the gym doors. My chest buzzed worse when Coach Williams opened the door. He was in a T-shirt and shorts. He shivered against the winter wind.

"Good to see you guys. Hurry up and get in here before I freeze."

I slipped inside and joined Gabe in peeling off my outer layers and lacing up my sneakers. Coach tossed me a ball and I warmed up slowly, dribbling between my legs and around my back, feeling the ball spring back to my fingertips. It had been too long.

Gabe caught a pass from Coach. "Did I ever tell you this guy was my hero when I was a kid?" he asked me. "Demarco Williams, meanest step back on the east coast. He was usually working out at the Y when he wasn't lighting it up in high school and university, and he'd always make time for kids like me who followed him around. I spent hours practicing this shot."

Gabe fired a step-back jumper and let his hand dangle in the air as the ball swished through the net.

Coach laughed. "Guess I taught you well."

It was strange at first, the three of us in the gym at night, but the tightness in my chest faded as Coach and Gabe joked and talked about Coach's college days. We ran through some shooting drills, then played a couple rounds of Twenty-one. I was wiped after an hour, which was frustrating. I used to be able to run forever. Still, being sweaty-tired felt better than the heavy exhaustion I felt lying in my room. I was glad Gabe made me do this.

"Your shot looks great as ever," Coach said as we rested against the stage. "I still wish you'd shoot more in games. We'll keep working on that when you're ready to come back."

My chest clenched again. "You still want me on the team?"

"Brian, of course," Coach said. "I wouldn't cut you if you sprained your ankle. I'd help you work back into game shape when you were healed enough to play. This isn't all that different. Come to practice when you're ready—whether it's tomorrow, next week, whenever. And I'm here around seven most mornings, so you can start the school day by shooting around, if that would help."

I bit my lip. As much as I was dreading school, basketball was the one thing pulling me back. Tonight reminded me how much I missed having a ball in my hands and being part of the team. Maybe it was somewhere I could be more than a useless sack of sadness.

I glanced at the clock on the gym wall. "You're still here tonight and you're back by seven? Do you live in the gym, Coach?"

He and Gabe laughed. Cracking a joke felt good too.

"Why are you doing all this for me?" I asked. "I mean, I appreciate it, but you have to deal with, like, every kid in this school."

Coach was quiet for a long time. "My college roommate was the best teammate you could ever ask for. He played his heart out every time he was on the floor. And in the gym, you'd have sworn he was the happiest guy on earth." Coach rubbed his forehead. "But when he was done playing, after his senior year . . ."

He paused, long enough that I knew the story didn't have a happy ending.

"I wish we'd talked more about life outside of basketball," Coach said quietly. "I wish I'd asked more often how he was doing. Now that I'm a teacher and a coach, I don't want anyone to think they have to suck it up and play or pretend they're fine when they're not."

He looked right at me. "You're a great kid, Brian. If there's anything I can do, you let me know, OK? I want to see you keep shooting."

I nodded again. My throat had gone tight.

We packed up and said good night to Coach. When Gabe pulled into my driveway, I thanked him for taking me out.

"Of course," he said, giving my shoulder a squeeze. "Love you, B."

"Love you too," I replied.

After the workout and a hot shower, I felt good enough to text Ezra a simple hey. I thought about texting other things too, like how are you or I miss you. Maybe tonight we could just talk, like I hadn't been able to in weeks, and things would feel normal again. Maybe Ezra could even talk me into attempting school again. But the minutes ticked by, and half an hour later he still hadn't written back. My courage faded. Maybe I'd spend one more day at home after all.

16. THE SECRET LINGO OF MUSIC GEEKS

EZRA

Victor was in my room. I didn't know why it felt so weird. I mean, things with Victor had always been complicated, but we were just working on music. It was like being partners on a school project.

He looked around at my posters. "Cool room. I've only heard of half these bands. You listen to a lot of music, don't you?"

I shrugged. "All the time, yeah."

He gave me one of those looks where I had no idea what he was thinking, and I wondered if this was going to be one big awkward mistake.

"Where should I set up?" he asked.

"Uh, how about over here." I cleared a space on my desk. Then I tuned my guitar while he ran a cable and a microphone to my amp. When he was done, he sat in my desk chair and spun around to face me.

"I tried a couple things," I said. "I can play them and see what you like."

"Cool." He pressed play on his computer. Suddenly this was more nerve-racking than when I was messing around on my own. It was still Victor's song. What if he hated my ideas?

I started with a simple riff that gathered steam as the song went along. Then I turned on my delay pedal and the notes I was playing cascaded into each other like a wave washing up on the beach. I risked a glance at Victor. His face was as still as ever. When I finished, he was silent.

"I like that a lot," he finally said. "But I think it might be too much for this song."

"Oh. Yeah, sure. Of course." I fiddled with my pedal as an excuse not to look at him.

"It's cool, though. We should still record it. You could build a song around it. Let's do that first."

When I looked up, he was opening a new file.

"I'll give you a click track to help you stay on beat," he said.

I huffed like I was offended. "Are you suggesting I don't have perfect rhythm?"

"OK, rock star." Victor smiled. Then he was back to business. "Ready?"

I nodded, and Victor hit record. I was more nervous now that it was just me and a steady click and Victor watching while he absently kept time with his foot. I started out fine, but I screwed up when I turned on the delay effect. I clicked my pedal a half beat too late and suddenly I was out of sync with the click track. The notes piled up into a mess. I stopped.

"Shoot," I said, embarrassed.

Victor shrugged. "The first half's great. We can keep it and start from the delay part." I must have still looked bummed, because he added, "I had to do my drum part like eight times."

We tried another take, but it still didn't feel right. I asked Victor if we could go again.

"That sounded perfect," he said after my third take. "Want to hear it?"

He hit play, and I moved closer to hear better. I'd recorded a few covers on my phone, though I never showed them to anyone. I didn't feel ready to put stuff online, like Kevan kept suggesting. But this was different. The music coming out of Victor's computer was mine.

"This is great," he said. "You could definitely make something out of it."

His voice was so close, it surprised me. I'd drifted so I was leaning over his shoulder.

I straightened up. "Uh, cool. Thanks for recording it."

"If you want to come to my place tomorrow, we could add some other parts." He tapped his laptop. "I've got all the software on here, but I like working with my actual keyboard. I'm more creative that way."

I rolled my eyes. "OK, rock star."

"Heh."

"That would be cool, though," I said. "I have basketball practice after school, but I could come to your place later. Do you want to work on your song now?"

He saved my guitar part and opened his song again. I played another part I made up, where I used my volume pedal to make the notes swell and contract. Victor broke into the biggest grin I'd seen from him yet.

"OK, I love that." He pointed at my pedal. "Can you make those crescendos even bigger and then cut them off at the end, like—"

Victor tried to demonstrate what he wanted with exaggerated air-guitar motions.

I couldn't help snickering. "Do I have to make those faces while I'm doing it?"

He laughed. "Shut up. You get the idea, right?" I tried what he was suggesting, and his grin got bigger. "Yeah, that's awesome. Let's record it."

As we recorded, his head bobbed along with the beat. When we listened back, Victor suggested I play one section differently. I tried it, and he was right; it sounded better. As we played with more ideas, we slipped into music-geek lingo. Most of my friends would have glazed over at words like "crescendo" and "staccato" and "minor seventh," but with Victor, it was natural. Sometimes, we understood each other before we could even finish our sentences.

"Try that an octave higher, and maybe—"

"Oh yeah, if I did—"

"Exactly. Perfect."

Victor played the latest take. "I think that's the one," he said. Then his phone dinged, and he checked the message. "That's definitely the one, because my mom's here."

He packed his gear and I walked him to the door.

"Thanks for letting me play on your song," I said. "This was really fun."

"Thanks for doing it," he replied. "You're talented. We'll do your song tomorrow?"

"Cool." It felt weird to think of my little riff as a song. But maybe it could become one.

After Victor left, I wandered into the kitchen for a snack. Mom was there, smiling.

"What?" I asked.

She played innocent. "What do you mean?"

"You're smiling."

"I'm not allowed to smile?"

"It's a suspicious kind of smile."

Mom laughed. "I'm smiling because *you're* smiling. You look so happy. Is that because you spent all night playing music, or because of who you were playing music with?"

My head nearly burst into flames. "It was the music. We were recording. Victor's just . . . Victor."

"Whoever he is, it's nice to see you so cheery." Mom squeezed my shoulder.

Her smile was burned in my mind as I poured a bowl of cereal. Mom and Dad had been cool when I told them last summer that I was gay, but we didn't really talk about it. Mom hinting that maybe I liked Victor was awkward, but . . . not the worst, I guess? I was glad she was OK with the idea of me having a crush on a guy.

Victor wasn't that guy, though. Sure, he was talented, and good looking. And tonight was . . . well, kind of amazing. And I'd had that dream where—well, I didn't want to think about that. But there were at least a dozen reasons why me and Victor should never happen.

What was he, exactly? I couldn't even bring myself to call him a friend when Mom asked. But I was already looking forward to tomorrow.

I checked my phone as I ate. Brian had texted more than an hour ago: hey

Shoot. I'd promised I'd talk to him tonight. I'd forgotten.

Hey sorry I got distracted with music, I replied. I'm still up if you want to talk?

He didn't write back 'til I was brushing my teeth. Nah it's ok. ttyl

Want me to come over at lunch tomorrow? I wrote back.

Sure

The Frosted Flakes sat heavy in my stomach when I went to bed. My best friend was struggling, and I'd ditched him for the guy who made his life miserable last year. Victor seemed different, but it still felt like I was betraying Brian. I should be hanging out with Brian after practice instead of squeezing him in at lunch and going to Victor's later.

Except . . .

Except I wanted to make music with Victor more than I wanted to hang out with Brian.

It took me a long time to fall asleep.

17. TRYING

BRIAN

Maybe Dr. Bender was right about the seasonal part of why I felt so lousy. Even after my first decent sleep in weeks, waking in the dead-cold dark was like starting the day underground. Still, I rolled onto the floor to do push-ups and stomach crunches. I remembered how good it'd felt to be in the gym last night. I knew exercise helped. This was me, trying.

Afterward, I lay flat and caught my breath. I felt not-terrible, but my chest went tingly as soon as I started thinking about school.

Ezra had said he'd come over at lunch. I'd start with social contact. Baby steps.

The sounds of an escalating argument drew me to the kitchen, where I found Mom leaning over the table while Richie ate breakfast in his pajamas.

"What's going on?" I asked.

Richie chomped a spoonful of cereal. "I'm on strike," he answered with his mouth full.

"On strike from what?"

Mom sighed. "He says he's not going to school."

Richie slurped his milk. "If Brian's skipping, I am too."

Mom looked from me to Richie. Her conflict was obvious: She wanted to lecture Richie that I wasn't skipping, but she didn't want to make excuses for me either. She wanted me out of the house. They both did.

I had to hand it to Richie. This was a smart play.

"Makes sense to me," I said. "Rich deserves a day off."

Mom sighed. "Brian—"

"Good. I'm staying home." Richie folded his arms.

Mom turned toward the sink. As she gathered herself, the silence was louder than a swarm of wasps. She probably wanted to tell Richie to knock it off and just go to school, but we all knew there was no moving him when he dug in. And it seemed like he was ready for war.

The other thing we all knew: I could fix this in a second. All I needed to do was leave the house. Get over myself. Stop stressing out Mom and Richie. Stop bringing everybody down.

I wished I could.

Mom reached for the notepad by the fridge where we wrote grocery lists.

"What are you doing?" Richie asked.

Mom didn't speak until she finished and dropped the list on the table.

"Since you're both staying home, here are your chores. Brian, you're in charge. If they're not finished when I get home, you lose your phone."

Before I could protest, she was already moving to the living room. Richie shot me a look, like *Did we just break Mom?* He followed her. She was sticking his Switch in her purse.

"What are you doing?" Richie gasped.

"This is coming with me. No video games. If you finish your list, you can work on your book talk that's due on Friday. Brian can help you."

"But—"

"Enjoy your day off. I still have to work." Mom marched down the hall and disappeared into the bathroom.

Richie stood there with his mouth open.

"Still want to stay home with me?" I asked.

His face scrunched up, and for a second I worried he was going to cry.

"Remember when you weren't a jerk and actually cared about me?" he snapped. Then he stomped to his room and slammed the door.

I thought about following him to apologize for . . . I didn't know. Being me, I guess. But I didn't. I poured a glass of water and swallowed my morning pill.

I rattled the bottle before putting it back on the shelf. I wondered when—or if—this ritual would make a difference. Felt like a whole lot of nothing so far.

A moment later, Richie emerged from his room, fully dressed. He headed to the front door and pulled on his coat.

"I'm going to school," he yelled. "Then I'm going to Leo's. I'll be home after dinner. Maybe."

He was out the door before Mom reached the kitchen. She stared at me.

"What?" I asked. "You won. Congratulations."

Mom's eye roll told me she was also remembering a time when I wasn't a jerk. "I have a bus to catch. I still expect those chores done. Goodbye, Brian."

A minute later, she was out too, and I was alone again. *My family's sick of me.*

A wave of anger welled up inside me. *Where do they get off being annoyed with me? I carried this family for months, and that's probably what messed me up in the first place.*

It was a monstrous thought, but I couldn't make it go away. So I tried to drown it out by blasting Vince Staples in my earbuds while I vacuumed the house. I'd never admit it to Mom—especially not right now—but cleaning felt better than moping in my room. The acoustics in the bathroom were excellent as I rapped along while scrubbing the sink.

When I finished and passed through the kitchen, I saw Richie's lunch bag. He'd forgotten it in his rush to leave.

I didn't think he really believed I didn't care about him. He just knew it would make me feel guilty.

It had worked. He was such a turd.

With a sigh, I packed his lunch and some other things in my backpack and risked going outside. It wasn't a terrible day for January—cold but sunny with no wind. My breath tightened when I reached the elementary school, and I felt silly for being so anxious. I rang the bell, and the secretary let me into the office. She'd worked at the school when I went here too, and she greeted me with a smile.

"Brian Day? Nice to see you! My goodness, you've gotten tall!"

"Hi, Ms. Cardillo. I'm dropping off Richie's lunch. He forgot it this morning."

"Ah." She *tsked* in sympathy. She knew what I was dealing with when it came to that kid. "And how's junior high treating you? You're off this morning?"

"Yeah, I, uh . . . it's been a morning." That was the kind of thing people said when they didn't want to explain.

Mrs. Cardillo said, "Mmm" like she understood. "I'll make sure Richie gets his lunch. And I'll tell him to thank his big brother. He's lucky to have you."

I managed a smile and headed back outside. I breathed the crisp air and pulled my backpack straps tight. My own lunch was in there, along with my basketball gear. I'd made it this far. Might as well keep trying, right? What was the worst that could happen?

Worst-Case Scenarios: Return to School Edition
4. *I'll have another panic attack in the hall.*
5. *This one will be worse and I'll accidentally poop my pants and become an outcast forever.*
6. *I'll have an actual heart attack, and the school will hang a memorial plaque in the spot where I dropped dead.*
7. *A hungry bear will wander into the schoolyard and eat me before I reach the door.*

On the walk to Halifax North, I texted Ezra and Mrs. Clelland. When the lunch bell sounded, I slipped in the back door and headed for Mrs. Clelland's room, hanging back as the stragglers from a seventh-grade class wandered out. When the coast was clear, I stepped inside.

Mrs. Clelland crossed the room toward me. "I just saw your text. I'm glad you're here. How are you feeling?"

I swallowed. "All right, I think."

"Can I get you anything?"

I shook my head. "I just want a quiet place for lunch, if that's OK."

She nodded and I took my usual seat near the window. A minute later, Ezra, Ty, and Kevan slipped in the door They approached cautiously.

Ty waved. "Hey, B."

"I'm not contagious," I said. "You can sit with me."

Ty rushed over and bear-hugged me from behind before I could get out of my chair.

"Maybe not *that* close," I squeezed out.

He laughed and let me go. They all sat. For a moment, we were quiet.

"Just act like it's a normal lunch," I said. "I probably won't talk much, but—"

"Like a normal lunch," Kevan joked. And just like that, it wasn't weird.

Well, it mostly wasn't weird. Kevan and Ty told stories and goofed around. But Ezra was quiet. He kept looking at me and then looking away, like he was checking on me but trying not to be obvious about it. I managed a smile to let him know I wasn't a complete mess. Not right now, anyway.

English was my only class today after lunch, so I didn't have to move. When the bell rang, Kevan headed to his next class, and other kids filed into the room. My chest tightened as I sensed my classmates looking at me, but Ezra and Ty formed a shield around me and nobody asked any questions.

It felt like the longest English period ever, but I survived. Finally, the bell rang. Mrs. Clelland gave me a tiny smile—nothing too obvious, just enough to let me know she was proud of me—and probably happy I didn't pass out.

"You coming to practice?" Ty asked. I nodded, and he grinned. He and Ezra flanked me in the hall, my personal bodyguards escorting me to the gym. Coach Williams greeted me with a big smile. I changed quickly and was warming up with Ezra and Ty by the time most of my teammates arrived.

"Spicy B!" Andre exclaimed, and everyone gave me fist bumps. Harrison nodded, like, *Great, you're back,* but he didn't say anything.

Practice went OK. Everyone was nice to me—almost too nice. They said, "Good job, B" when I did the simplest things right. It was like no one wanted to upset me in case I fell apart. I hated seeming this fragile. Still, I was glad to be there. Being in the gym made me feel more focused, less swamped by everything. And I wasn't at my best but I didn't suck, either. When we scrimmaged at the end of practice, I hit a three-pointer over Ezra, and later I stole the ball from

Jayden and threw a no-look pass to Andre for the game-winning layup.

As I changed afterward, exhaustion hit me. I pulled on my hoodie and zoned out for a minute. Ty said goodbye, and then Ezra was the only one left with me. I snapped out of my daze and reached for my boots.

Ezra tugged on his backpack. "So, um, how was that? Do you feel OK?"

I knew he was asking because he cared, but I wished all our conversations weren't about my mental state. "I'm tired, but fine. What's new with you?"

Ezra adjusted his glasses. "Uh . . . I've been working on some music lately."

"Yeah? For the talent show?"

"Maybe. I don't know. I'm still not sure what to play." He tucked his hands in his pockets. "Want me to walk you home?"

"Nah, I'm OK. I'll see you tomorrow."

It came out automatically, and Ezra's eyes widened with hope. "Are you coming all day?"

I swallowed. "I'll try, I guess."

"Cool. See you then."

"Yeah. Uh, thanks." I gave him a hug. He seemed surprised before he hugged me back.

A memory popped into my mind from the summer, a lazy August day at Ty's where we'd goofed around in his pool and then sat on his deck playing cards and laughing long after dark. At the end of the night, I'd given Ezra a big hug because I was so grateful to have actual friends who made hanging out so *easy*.

I wondered if it would ever feel that easy again.

We split up and I headed back into the cold. I tried to focus on the positive, like how I made it through the afternoon without any disasters. But I kept coming back to how everyone was tiptoeing around me. Even Ezra was fidgety, like he was afraid to say the wrong thing.

I dug out my phone to distract me before I went to dark places, but my heart sped up when I saw four texts and two missed calls from Mom.

I scrolled through the texts, and my fear turned into annoyance.

Hi, just checking in. How's your day so far?

Brian?

Can you send me a quick reply?

Just want to make sure everything's good

I closed the app. Nothing was wrong; Mom was just paranoid about me too. I was about to tuck my phone away when she called again. I was tempted to ignore it, but I answered. "Yeah?"

She sighed in relief, then tried to sound upbeat. "Just seeing how your day's going."

"It's fine. You didn't have to call every ten minutes."

Another sigh, but this one was different. "Well, you didn't answer—"

"I couldn't check my phone in class, or during practice."

Long pause. "You went to school?"

"For the afternoon, yeah."

More silence. *Was she trying not to cry?*

"Anyway, I'm walking and it's cold, so I'll talk to you later."

"Brian—"

"Bye, Mom." I hung up.

Even though I was drained, I walked home in record time, fueled by my irritation. Richie wasn't home—probably at Leo's. I was glad. I was ready to be alone.

18. UPSIDE-DOWN VICTOR

EZRA

Mom kept smiling at dinner. "You look nice," she said.

"Big plans this evening?" Dad asked.

I swallowed. "Just going to Victor's."

Sure, I'd showered after practice, and I'd put gel in my hair to give my curls a boost, but I *always* looked fresh when I went out. I didn't do anything extra.

"Victor? Is that the boy who was here last night?" Dad asked.

"He's a *musician*," Mom said, with more emphasis than she needed.

"We were recording," I said. "That's what we're doing tonight too. Victor's a great piano player. You should hear him play 'Moonlight Sonata.'"

Dad's eyes lit up. He was usually so laid-back, he was like a walking nap, but he loved classical music. I'd never seen him more excited than when I'd helped him set up a Bluetooth speaker at his orthodontist practice so he could stream concertos all day. I figured if I could shift the conversation to music, maybe Mom would lay off with . . . whatever she was doing. I raced through the rest of dinner to avoid any more Victor-related questions.

I still felt weird about going to his place. I couldn't even be honest with Brian when he asked what I'd been up to lately. I hadn't *lied*, but I'd practically ran away so I didn't have to say, "Actually, I'm hanging out with your former bully."

I couldn't shake my nagging guilt, so I texted Kevan.

Me: Can I ask a weird question?
Kevan: Strange weird or gross weird?
Me: Not gross. Is Victor still mean to you like last year?
Kevan: Not really. Why?
Me: Just curious. He seems different now
Kevan: Yeah way different. So much quieter. Not shy like Brian, but . . .
It's hard to explain. It's weird
Me: Good weird or bad weird?
Kevan: I don't know.
Good that he stopped being a jerk, obviously.
But it's spooky
Like he came out of the woods a different person
Me: The woods?
Kevan: There's a rumor that he went missing this summer

Apparently he nearly died, like he almost
drowned or something
That's why he didn't come to school til later
No one knows the real story except Colby, but he
won't tell. I tried

Victor had almost *died*? I wondered if any of that was
true. All I could write back was WOW

Kevan: No kidding. Maybe he was trapped in the
Upside Down
He's part shadow monster now

Kevan threw in a laughing emoji. But it wasn't something I feel like joking about, so I changed the subject.

Me: Do you talk to Colby much anymore?
Kevan: Sometimes. It's not like it used to be, though
Do you miss hanging out with him?

A wave of memories hit me. Sleepovers, snack runs,
silly pranks, laughing so hard we couldn't catch our breath.
I swallowed hard. Sometimes

Me too, Kev responds.
I'd just said bye to Kevan when my phone rang.
"Hey Madi, what's up?" I answered.
"Hi Ezra." She took a breath. "I've been thinking about
what to play at the talent show."
"Yeah, same. I'm having a hard time choosing."

"I was too, but I've decided. I'd really like to sing 'Blackbird.' And you played it so well at our recital last June . . . I'm wondering if you'd accompany me."

Madi's request caught me by surprise.

Before I could answer, she added, "You should do your own thing too. But I'd love to have you play with me."

"Yeah, I'd be happy to," I said.

"Great, thank you!" I could hear the smile in her voice. "This is going to be such a great show. I can't wait."

"Yeah," I agreed. "Hey, random question. You know how you said Victor disappeared over the summer—do you think something bad happened?"

Madi huffed. "I've heard rumors. But he probably made half of them up himself. Who knows what's real with him. Why?"

My face heated up. "I don't know. I've been talking to him lately about music and the talent show and stuff . . . and I can't really figure him out."

That sentence was at least two-thirds true.

"Well, you shouldn't waste your time," Madi said. "You can't trust him."

"Thanks for the tip." I said goodbye without mentioning that I was heading to his house in five minutes.

Mom dropped me off at Victor's apartment building near the Common, which was a long way from my neighborhood.

My mouth went dry as he buzzed me in and I took the elevator to the seventh floor. I knocked on 712. Victor came to the door in a tank top and shorts, even though it was freezing outside.

"I should have warned you," he said. "It's always hot in here."

I slipped off my shoes and hung up my coat. "Have you lived here long?"

"Only since August." I followed him to the living room, and he introduced me to his mom, who was reading on the couch. Then he led me to his room.

His beige walls were bare and there was hardly anything on his dresser or desk, other than a laptop and some cables stretching to a keyboard and a set of speakers. It felt like he hadn't been there long—or maybe he kept things simple to match his inscrutable personality.

I sat on his bed. "Do you get a ride to school? That would be a long walk."

He fiddled with his laptop. "Mom usually drives me. Technically I should go to Central. But I tried it and didn't like it, so I transferred back to North. I used Dad's address. He still lives in our old house."

I hesitated. "So, your parents—"

"They split up this summer."

"Oh. Sorry."

"Don't be. It's better this way."

Now I was curious about his family. Back when we still talked, Colby told me Victor had two older brothers. They hung out with Colby's brother Jackson, and Colby said they were even meaner than Jackson, which meant they were awful. This was a two-bedroom apartment, so I guessed his brothers lived with his dad. I wondered if it was hard to have his family separated like that. I knew how much I missed Nat sometimes.

"You went to Central?" I asked. "Is that where you were until November?"

He half grinned. "Which story did you hear? My favorite's the one where I got abducted by aliens."

I knew he was joking, but there was something almost wistful in the way he said it.

He turned in his chair. "Anyway, I started messing around with your guitar riff after school. You can tell me if you like it or not."

He hit play, and his room filled with music. Victor had added in some piano, a simple bass line, and a drum beat. I sat with my chin on my hands, listening. When it was done, I was quiet, thinking of what to say.

His eyebrows raised. "You don't love it."

"No, it's not that—"

"You can be honest, Ezra. You're bad at hiding what you're thinking."

"You should give me lessons, then," I shot back. "You're great at it."

His half smile returned. "So?"

I exhaled. "I like the piano part, but what if you used something softer, like a synth? And the drums could be more . . . I'm not sure how to describe it."

"Show me." Victor clicked his mouse, then waved me to the keyboard. He played a few keys. "There's your bass drum, snare, hi hat, whatever you want."

I sat at the keyboard and played around. I felt self-conscious with Victor watching, and it took a few minutes to figure out the beat I wanted. It was looser than what Victor had recorded, more hip-hop.

"I see what you're going for," he said.

I frowned. "It's still not quite right, though. Do you have other drum kits on there?"

"Sure." He scrolled through kits until he landed on one where the bass and snare hit with a satisfying *boom-bap*.

I sat up. "That's it. Let's try this one."

Victor recorded me playing the new beat. When I finished and we played it back, he nodded. "That's tight. But yeah, the piano doesn't fit. And we need a better bass line. Let me try something."

Like last night at my house, the initial awkwardness evaporated as we started bouncing ideas back and forth. I took off my sweater, because he wasn't lying, his room was boiling. We slid between the keyboard and the laptop, and Victor showed me how to adjust settings and patches in his software program. Once we were satisfied with the recorded parts, we hunched over the laptop, sitting shoulder to shoulder as we mixed the volume and added some effects. Victor kept glancing at me.

"What?" I asked.

He grinned. "Your hair smells like coconut. It's making me hungry."

My face heated up. "I used gel after I showered. I had practice after school." I didn't want him thinking I showered just for him.

He leaned one elbow on the desk. "Coconut gel. So that's the secret to your cool hair."

I adjusted my glasses. "That and genetics. You can't eat my hair, though."

Victor said, "Heh."

"I like how you let your hair grow longer, by the way," I said. "It looks good on you."

"Thanks."

Victor was still leaning against his desk with an almost-smile. My mind raced. *He complimented my hair. I complimented his hair. Why's he looking at me like that? What's happening right now? And why is it so blazing hot in here?*

Victor's phone buzzed on his desk. He left it until it buzzed two more times. He rolled his eyes and picked it up.

"Colby. Math homework meltdown. He can wait."

Colby. Now I was imagining the dozens of texts and jokes they'd shared since the last time Colby said more than *Hey* to me.

I stood up. "You can write him back. I have to go to the bathroom."

I slipped out and found the bathroom. My mind was spinning with all the reasons it felt wrong to hang out with Victor, but I was also thinking about how he'd looked at me, and how I liked it, and how natural it felt when we were making music, and . . .

I think I have a crush on him.

When I left the bathroom, his mom was in the kitchen, pouring a glass of wine.

"Can I get you a drink?" she asked, then glanced at her glass. "Not this, obviously."

"Water would be great, thanks," I said.

She filled two glasses. "You sound good in there. I'm glad Victor has someone to make music with. It's his favorite thing in the world right now."

She glanced toward his room, and I saw the same worried mom look I saw from Brian's mom sometimes.

"He's really talented," I said.

"Yes, he is. Anyway, I won't keep you. Enjoy your recording."

When I returned to Victor's room, he was setting down his phone. "Problem solved. Colby will survive." He studied my face as I handed him a glass. "Are you OK?"

"I'm fine."

He raised an eyebrow. "Remember how you're bad at hiding what you're thinking?"

My heart went fluttery. I had to say something. "This isn't weird for you?"

His forehead wrinkled. "Weird?"

"I like making music with you," I said. "But I'm best friends with Brian, and you bullied him all last year. And I *used* to be best friends with Colby, who changed after he started hanging out with you, and now he barely talks to me. I can't just pretend none of that ever happened."

Victor's face went blank. "So you don't want to do this anymore?"

"No, no. I just think we should talk about stuff."

"So you want an excuse why it's OK to hang out with a jerk like me."

"That's not what I said." His sarcasm stung. Suddenly this felt too hard. I reached for my sweater and stood up. "Never mind, I should go."

"Ezra, wait. I didn't mean that." Victor sighed and pushed back his hair. "Saying mean stuff is this habit that . . . it's like . . ." His face flushed, and he looked toward the window. "I'm seeing a therapist now. I haven't told many people. Everyone talks about me enough already."

I sat back down. "I won't tell anyone. But you shouldn't be embarrassed about going to therapy. That's good."

He tugged at the hem of his tank top. "Colby and I started hanging out in class last year. I wasn't trying to steal him."

I folded my arms. "I know. He ghosted me after I told him I'm gay. That's on him."

Victor nodded. "I get why you're mad at him. But he stuck with me when everyone else bailed. And he knows he messed up with you."

"If he's actually sorry, he knows how to find me." My neck felt prickly, and I didn't want to talk about Colby anymore. "What about Brian? Why were you so mean to him?"

Victor winced. "I'm not proud of last year, all right?" He lowered his eyes and traced little circles on his desk.

"I believe you, but you didn't answer my question. And you've never apologized." My voice went shaky. "I feel like I'm lying to Brian. He doesn't know we're hanging out. If we're going to be friends, or music partners, or whatever we're doing, it would help if you'd at least say sorry to him."

My face was on fire. I rubbed my eyes under my glasses. I hated that I was getting emotional. Victor was right: I was terrible at hiding my feelings. And he was the opposite. His ears were red, but he stared at his computer, not looking at me, not saying anything. It was kind of irritating.

How could one person make me feel so many different things at once?

My phone dinged, and I checked the message. "My mom's on her way. I have to go."

"Are you together?" Victor asked.

"What?"

"You and Brian. You seem really close. Just wondering if you're, like, *together*."

"Like a couple? No. But he's my best friend. I care about him a lot."

"I know." There was something almost sad in the way Victor said it.

He walked me to his apartment door, and we said an awkward goodbye. He didn't ask if we were going to do this again. I didn't know if I wanted him to ask. I didn't know what to think as I walked toward the elevators. Behind me, his door clicked shut.

19. GOBLIN MODE

BRIAN

A week after my public meltdown, I walked to school in the dark and shot around with Coach before class. It mellowed me out enough that I made it through the day without panicking. So I did it again on Monday. And for the rest of the week.

Mom said she was proud of me for working so hard. I grunted.

This became my life: Gym. Class. Practice or a game. Nap. Dinner. Homework. Bed. Repeat. I saw Dr. Bender once a week. I sat with my friends in school, tried to be social, but it was all one big ball of bleh. January stretched on forever.

After slogging through a few weeks, everything on Earth started getting on my nerves.

An Incomplete List of Things I Can't Stand
The sound of the school bell.
The way Ms. Virth says, "Good morning, citizens."
Icy sidewalks. Cold weather. Everything about winter.

How Kevan ends sentences with "ya know?" (I hadn't noticed until recently; now I hate it.)
Ezra's I'm worried about you face.
The school cafeteria—the noise, the smell, people's voices, everything.
Literally anything my mom does.

Dealing with school all day was irritating, but being home with Mom wasn't any better. The smallest things drove me bonkers, like when she talked to herself, or turned the pages in a book too loudly, or left the hall light on so the glow shone under my bedroom door.

I still hadn't visited Dad since Christmas. We'd talked on the phone, but it wasn't the same. I was a terrible son, but I couldn't help it. It was like I'd been cursed by an evil wizard. Regular Brian was trapped in the basement of my brain, forced to watch Cursed Monster Brian stomp on everything.

I couldn't explain this to Mom, or my friends. But I told Dr. Bender about the monster curse in the first week of February.

"Interesting theory," she offered. "Have you run afoul of any sorcerers lately? Stolen any artifacts with evil powers?"

I shrugged. "I've always wondered if my French teacher is into the dark arts."

Dr. Bender pondered this. "French teachers have been known to practice the occult."

My weekly talks with Dr. Bender were like a release valve. I eased into her couch, and it reminded me how tense I'd been from holding in my nastiest thoughts.

"I know you can't answer this, but when will everything stop sucking so much?" I asked. "Shouldn't the pills be helping by now?"

She nodded sympathetically. "This is the frustrating stage, right? You're doing all the right things, but you don't feel like it's making a difference."

"Yeah."

"Well, I see a difference. You have more energy than you did a month ago."

"Sure, but it's evil rage energy. First I was miserable, then I barely felt anything, and now I'm constantly angry."

"I know it's not a fun place to be, but this isn't always a journey that moves in a straight line, I'm afraid. Try to acknowledge what you're feeling, without judging yourself for it." Dr. Bender sipped her tea. "You said something in January that stuck with me. You mentioned that you felt like you were letting everyone down. Do you still feel that way?"

I thought for a while. "I guess so. I'm keeping up with homework and friends and stuff, but I'm still a drag to be around. And I haven't visited Dad in weeks."

"Often, the people we care about have more grace and patience for us than we imagine," Dr. Bender said. "I know it's not easy, but try to show yourself some of that grace and patience too."

"Yeah . . . I'll try."

"Fair enough. Is there anything that does give you life right now?"

I could only think of one. "Basketball."

"That's good. Keep playing."

I did. I'd live in the gym if I could. I shot in the mornings, and after practice I hung around until Coach was ready to go home. If Gabe wasn't busy, sometimes we'd find an open court after dinner and play some more. It kept me from losing it completely. But another thing happened: All that practice kept making me better.

★★★

Our first playoff game was against Fairview, the team that beat us before Christmas. Their starting shooting guard, a kid named Jake, gave me a smirk before tipoff that let me know he remembered my meltdown in that game.

Jake came out hot and hit two quick three-pointers. Three minutes into the game, we were down 10–3 and Coach called timeout.

"Come on, y'all," Ty pled in our huddle. "We can't lose to these guys again. This is the playoffs."

"We need to slow Jake down," Coach said. "He's getting too many open looks."

"Let me guard him, Coach," I said. "I'll stop him. I promise."

Everyone looked at me. I didn't usually say much in timeouts.

Coach nodded. "He's yours, Brian. Run him off the three-point line and try to trap him on screens." He surveyed the huddle. "Everyone else, be ready to help. And challenge them more on offense. We're settling for outside shots. Get to the rim."

The referee blew her whistle, and we headed back to the court. Jake smirked again when he saw me coming.

"Hope you can keep your cool this time."

I didn't say anything. I just glared at him.

When his teammate threw him a pass, I picked it off and raced to our hoop for a layup.

Ty gave me a high-five. "That's it, B. Make him work."

Jake darted around the court, but I stayed glued to him like I was his reflection. He was quick, but I was just as fast, and my arms were longer. I was also running on evil rage energy. The only thing I cared about was stopping him and winning the game. I stole the ball from him twice more and forced him into heaving tough shots that clanked off the rim. I even blocked him twice.

"He's fouling me," Jake complained to the ref after I swatted his shot out of bounds.

She shook her head. "That's good defense."

I didn't say a word. I just kept hounding him.

He didn't make another three-pointer all game. I hit two in the second half as we pulled away and won easily, 58–39.

In the post-game huddle, everyone was hyped that we were going to the next round of the playoffs. Coach held up his hand for quiet. Then he looked at me.

"That's maybe the best defensive game we've played all year. You all played well, but Brian set the tone today. Well done."

The hollering started up again. Andre thumped my chest. "You were *mean* out there, man."

I changed quickly and left the gym with Ezra and Ty. As we were walking out, Ezra tucked his hands in his pockets.

"We should celebrate or something. Want to come over?"

I shrugged. "I should get home. Mom's working and I need to pick up Richie from Kevan's." This wasn't exactly true. The Sidhus didn't mind letting Richie stay, and he was happier there than at home with me.

Ezra's face fell. "Oh. OK. Talk to you later?"

"Sure."

Ty tilted his head. "You good, B?"

I pulled up my hood. "Just tired."

"Makes sense. You worked your butt off. You were all the way in that kid's head." He patted my shoulder.

As I started toward home, Ty and Ezra watched me go before they headed off together. In his cell in the basement of my brain, Regular Brian was saying, *Turn around. Go with your friends.* But Cursed Monster Brian kept walking.

I shouldn't have been so angry. I had a great game, and we'd won. But I still felt full of knives.

If I can't be happy now, how am I ever going to be happy?

I stopped at the Sidhus', though I didn't know why I bothered. Richie made a stink like I'd expected.

"They said I could stay for supper," he protested. "We're having chicken stew."

Mrs. Sidhu smiled at me. "You're welcome to stay too, Brian. Please, come in."

Dinner smelled delicious. Everything the Sidhus cooked was delicious.

But I shook my head. "I just played basketball, and I really need a shower."

She laughed, a warm, lilting sound. "Don't be silly. It's not like we've never smelled a teenage boy around here. Right, Kevan?"

Kevan wrinkled his nose as he walked into the kitchen. "Are you calling me stinky, Mom? That's low. Hey, Brian. Did you win?"

"Yeah, by a bunch."

"Wow, don't sound so excited," Kevan teased. "Are you staying for dinner?"

I shook my head. "You can stay, Rich. I'm going to head home."

"We have plenty of stew," Mrs. Sidhu said. "And fresh naan. Come, eat. It'll do you good."

"Yeah, come on," Richie said. "Please?"

They were all watching me. Richie gave me his puppy dog eyes. He actually wanted me here. He'd even said *please*. It smelled so good here.

Stay, Regular Brian screamed from his cell.

"I, um . . ."

Stay.

"Thanks, but I have homework and, uh, I'm going to go."

Before anyone could talk me out of it, before the aroma of spices could win me over, before Richie could grab my arm and drag me back inside, I slipped out the door.

★★★

It started snowing, falling fast in thick flakes that clung to my eyelashes and burrowed under my collar. I was chilled and damp by just the short walk home.

Our house was dark.

I shouldn't be here.

Mom wouldn't be home for an hour, at least. I should have been eating at the Sidhus' or hanging out at Ezra's— anywhere but here, alone.

But I didn't want to be around anyone. Not when I was like this.

Maybe I really was cursed. An awful chant kept running through my head.

You'll never get through this.

You'll never feel better.

You'll never be happy again.

I made some peanut butter toast, hoping some food would help, but it only reminded me of what I was missing at Kevan's. I took a hot shower, but that only felt good until I turned off the water and goose bumps sprung up on my wet skin.

The chant grew louder.

You'll never get through this.

You'll never feel better.

You'll never be happy again.

By the time I finished dressing, I couldn't stand it anymore. Not the voice of doom in my head, not the itching restless anger in my chest, not the thought of feeling this way again tomorrow, and the next day, and the next. It all felt so suffocating.

I didn't know if I could keep doing this.

Pulling on my boots was automatic, like I was on cruise control. Regular Brian pled that this was a bad idea, but Cursed Monster Brian was in control. I had no idea where I was going, only that I couldn't stay in the house. The walls were collapsing on me.

I knew I should walk to Kevan's, or Ezra's. Somewhere safe. But I didn't know if I could bring myself to do it.

I kept thinking about how easy it would be to get lost in the snow.

Stay, Regular Brian begged, and this time it sounded like a warning.

I was pulling on my coat when I heard voices and thumping outside. Then the door swung open, and Richie, Kevan, Ezra, and Ty piled inside. Their coats were white with snow and they were laughing, but they stopped when they saw me.

"Brian?" Richie said. "Where are you going?"

"Uh . . . just for a walk. I need some air."

Ty brushed snow from his hair. "It's awful out. You don't want to be out there."

"So why are *you* all here?" It came out sharp, but they didn't react.

Kevan held up a grocery bag. "I brought stew. And cookies."

I sighed. "Guys—"

"This is not a discussion," Kevan cut me off. "You need to eat. And the Sidhus never let friends go hungry."

He pushed me toward the kitchen. I gave up and took off my coat. The entryway was a soggy mess as everyone jostled to shake off snow. Richie gave me a long stare as he brushed past.

Ezra was watching me too. He hadn't said anything yet.

Kevan made himself at home in our kitchen, filling a bowl with stew. "Eat," he commanded. "While it's still warm."

He wasn't going to take no for an answer, and my toast hadn't done much, so I sat and ate. It was delicious, of course—rich and spicy, the perfect food for a snowy night. Each bite was like swallowing a hug. As I stuffed my face, Ty told Richie and Kevan about our game.

"This guy was a beast." He poked my shoulder. "Spicy B is an all-star defender."

I knew it wasn't a coincidence that they'd all showed up at once. They could tell I was a mess, and they'd conspired to feed me.

Cursed Monster Brian was mad about it. *They talk about you behind your back. They're treating you like a baby.* But Regular Brian wanted to cry out of gratitude. *They haven't given up on you yet.*

It also hit me that they weren't just here for me. Ty and Kevan kept making Richie laugh, and Ezra slipped him another piece of naan. They were taking care of my brother, doing what I couldn't because Cursed Monster Brian wouldn't let me.

I didn't deserve these guys.

As I was finishing, Kevan turned to Richie. "Go play your Switch in your room for a bit, OK?"

Richie scowled. "If you're gonna talk to Brian, I'm staying."

"We need to have a grown-folks conversation, Rich," Ty said. He made a silly face, but Richie didn't laugh.

"You're not grown folks; you're in junior high!"

Then Kevan whispered in his ear, and Richie finally shrugged. "All right, deal." He rose slowly, giving me another long stare before heading to his room.

"What did you tell him?" I asked once he was gone.

"That's confidential." Kevan zipped his lips shut.

The kitchen went quiet then. I folded my arms. "So, is this an intervention?"

"Yes," Ezra said. "What's going on with you?"

I sighed. "You know what's going on. I'm depressed."

"Yeah, but you're supposed to tell us stuff, remember? Lately it's like you can't stand to be around us. Like you're not even trying to—"

"You think I'm not *trying?* Are you *kidding me?*" The words exploded out before I could stop them. Ezra flinched like I'd thrown hot stew in his face.

This was what I was afraid of: the moment when I couldn't hold Cursed Monster Brian back, and he hurt somebody. I buried my face in my hands. I couldn't bear to look at Ezra right now. I wished they'd all go away and leave me alone, like I deserved.

No. I don't want that at all.

"I'm sorry," I mumbled.

"You looked rough, B," Ty said. "That's why we came over. We didn't want you to be alone. You can tell us what's up."

I bit my lip. "I don't know. I'm just . . . *mad*. All the time."

"We know that part," Ty said. "I mean, your death glare is incredible."

I looked up. "You noticed?"

Kevan and Ty laughed.

"How could we *not* notice?" Kevan said. "Yesterday at lunch you almost burned a hole in my face."

My cheeks went hot. "Sorry."

Ty shrugged. "I'm sorry you're still feeling so lousy, but it's OK to show some attitude. You were a stone-cold killer in the game today. It was great."

I sighed. "Yeah, but . . ." I ran a hand through my hair in frustration as the words wouldn't come.

"No rush," Ezra said. "You can tell us when you're ready."

Kevan opened the tub of cookies, and we ate in silence. They were shortbread, buttery and crisp, with a hint of cardamom. Kev really was a genius.

If Dr. Bender walked into my kitchen right now, she'd boil the kettle and bring me tea, then she'd repeat what she'd told me in our last session: *"Often, the people we care about have more grace and patience for us than we imagine."*

I picked up a second cookie, then I blurted it out. "There's a monster in my brain."

They waited for me to explain, but I didn't know what else to say.

Ezra rubbed his chin. "Like the Green Goblin?"

Ty frowned. "What?"

"You know, from Spider-Man." Ezra hunched forward. "Remember when Norman Osborn argues with himself in the mirror 'cause the Green Goblin is taking over his mind?"

"Ah, I get it," Kevan agreed.

"I guess it's kind of like that," I said. "I didn't inject myself with super-serum. But I feel that way sometimes. Like I'm turning into a supervillain." I exhaled. "I don't want to be like this, and it doesn't feel like I'm getting better, and I just lose it sometimes."

"You're allowed to lose it sometimes," Ty said. "You can let out the death stare."

Kevan stretched. "Maybe you need to yell more. Like that time you cursed in the middle of a game. Let it out, ya know?"

"I'll keep that in mind, Kev," I said.

Ty's phone dinged, and he sighed. "My dad's here. He didn't want us walking home in the snow." He pushed back from the table. "Come on, guys. We'll give you a ride home."

Ezra reluctantly rose, and Kevan stood up too. I walked them to the door.

"Green Goblin should be our new code word," Kevan said as he pulled on his boots. "If you feel like you're going to snap, just say *Green Goblin* and we'll give you space or whatever."

"I like it," Ty said. "We got you. Even in Goblin Mode."

"Thanks, guys."

Ezra lingered until Kevan and Ty were out the door. He stared at his boots. "I didn't mean to say you're not trying."

"I know," I said. "Thanks for coming over. It helped."

"Really?"

"Yeah."

He hugged me good night. I watched as he trudged to Mr. Marsman's car. The snow on the front steps was a couple inches deep already, which meant I'd have to shovel later. *Great.* As Ty's dad backed out of the driveway, his tires spun before they gripped the road and he started slowly up the hill. I glanced at the sky and wondered how Mom was doing trying to get home by bus. She was usually back by now.

As I closed the door, I still felt knotted up inside. My friends had helped, but the goblin voice was still in the background, telling me I'd be stuck like this forever.

Maybe Kevan was right. Maybe yelling would drown it out.

I walked to the patio door and slid it open. On a whim, I pulled off my socks and stepped onto our tiny deck. My bare feet burned as they sunk into the snow. I took two more steps and stood there, focusing on the fire in my toes. I peeled off my hoodie and T-shirt and tossed them inside. The wind whipped snow against my bare chest, and I stretched my arms and yelled as loud as I could.

It felt not-terrible, so I kept yelling. It was just noise at first, then I added a few choice swear words, and that felt even better.

"What are you doing?"

Richie stood in the doorway, staring at me.

"Goblin therapy, Rich," I told him.

He leaned out into the cold. "Can I try?"

"Sure. You have lots to yell about too."

Richie was already barefoot—he never wore socks in the house, not even in winter—and he took off his shirt and stepped outside. He gasped when his feet touched the snow.

"Go ahead," I said.

He clenched his fists. "AAAAAH!"

Richie packed a snowball and hurled it at the backyard fence. Throwing snowballs seemed like an excellent addition to screaming, so I did the same. After we flung a few into the dark, Richie turned and fired one at my chest. It exploded all over me, stinging like a million icy needles pressing into my skin.

It was kind of amazing.

I threw one back at him. He twisted away and it hit him just above his butt.

"There's snow in my underwear!" He did a little dance of agony, then he rushed me, and we flung snow at each other and hollered and wrestled.

"Boys? What in the *world?!*" Mom stood in the doorway, bug-eyed. "I could hear you halfway down the street! Get in here before the neighbors call the police!"

Richie and I piled inside. We were bright pink from the cold. Mom looked me over like I'd lost it completely.

I turned to Richie. He grinned.

We flung ourselves at her. She shrieked as we dripped melting snow all over her. Then she laughed, and tickled Richie until he squirmed away. Finally she leaned against me and sighed.

It'd been a long time since I'd hugged my mom. When I let go, she swallowed hard.

"Brian, how are you doing?" she asked in a shaky voice.

"I don't really feel like talking," I said. "I'm going to go change. But there's chicken stew in the kitchen. Kevan brought some over."

"It's delicious," Richie added.

We left Mom and headed to our rooms. I was still shivering after I changed, so I climbed in bed with a book. A few minutes later, Richie showed up with a graphic novel. Without asking, or saying anything, he slid under the covers next to me. I let him stay.

20. REBOUND

EZRA

Real life was complicated enough, but my imagination didn't even give me a break when I was sleeping. When I jolted awake from another messy Victor-related dream, I peeked at my clock—it was ten minutes to midnight. After going to the bathroom, I was too awake to fall back asleep. I slipped on my bathrobe and headed upstairs. Mom was sitting at the kitchen island, illuminated by the glow of her laptop.

"You're still working?" I asked.

Mom looked up. "I was prepping for a court case, then I got tired and fell down a rabbit hole of online shopping." She lowered the laptop screen. "What are you doing up?"

I yawned. "I was asleep. Just woke up."

"Oh? Bad dream?"

My cheeks went warm. I didn't want to talk about my dream. "Sort of. I'm going to get some water and go back to bed."

"Ezra." She pulled out the stool beside her. "Is something on your mind? You seem a little off lately."

I sat beside her. I didn't talk much with my parents about *feelings* and stuff. Sometimes I did with Nat or Brittany, but I hadn't seen them much lately. They had their own busy lives.

I scratched my head. "I don't know. Brian's having a hard time, and I'm not sure how to help."

"You have such a big heart, Ezra." Mom smiled. "When you were younger, you'd come home spitting mad every time Colby's brother was mean to him. You've always cared so deeply about your friends."

I swallowed. "Colby and I aren't really friends anymore. He basically ghosted me after I told him I'm gay."

"Oh, honey." Mom's face fell. "I'm so sorry."

We sat quietly for a minute. I waited for Mom to say something comforting about Colby, or give me advice about Brian, but she didn't. She just squeezed my hand. I guess once you hit a certain age, there aren't any magic Mom words that fix everything.

"What about your musical friend?" she asked. "You two seem like you have a lot of *harmony*." She tried to keep a straight face, but she started giggling.

"Mom," I groaned. "That was awful."

"Sorry. It's late." She got herself under control and looked at me expectantly.

"Things with Victor are . . . complicated," I said.

We'd barely talked in the three weeks since I'd gone to his apartment. He'd sent me the finished version of my song with a three-word text: here you go. Then, silence. At school, he was always with Colby and their ninth-grade friends. We said "Hey" when we passed each other, but that was it.

I guess I shouldn't be shocked. Madi had warned me that he was like this. But sometimes when my chat app was open, I saw three dots pop up and then disappear, like Victor was starting a message but he didn't know what to say. I got it, because I'd done the same thing. And I still thought about playing music together all the time. And maybe some other things too.

"Friend complicated?" Mom hesitated. "Or romantic complicated?"

"I don't know. Maybe the second one." I rubbed my face. "When we're making music, it's like we have this connection. But then at school we barely talk. I don't even know if he likes me. Maybe he just likes recording. And he's so mysterious, like there's stuff he doesn't want to talk about at all. Anyway, I'm trying not to get my hopes up."

Mom sighed. "You know, when I was your age, I had a crush on this boy. Frankie Gallo. He was too cool. Looked like a young Ralph Tresvant."

"Who?"

Mom side-eyed me. "All that music you listen to, and you don't know Ralph Tresvant? New Edition?"

I shook my head.

"Boy, you're making me feel old." Mom laughed. Her Trini accent came out when she was joking, and I liked how musical it sounded. "Half the girls I knew had crushes on Frankie, though he barely talked to us. But one day he walked me home, and I felt like the most special girl in the neighborhood. He still ignored me at school, but I didn't care, because we had this secret. We'd walk home together every Tuesday, took the back way so no one saw us. At first we'd hold hands, then—"

"I get the picture, Mom!"

"Well, you can probably guess the rest too then. Eventually I realized that Frankie only walked with me on Tuesdays because he was walking with Charlene on Wednesdays and Kimi on Thursdays. That was my first lesson to watch out for boys who act aloof and mysterious." Mom sighed. "So you're already wiser than I was. But that doesn't make it easier, does it?"

"Not really."

She gently brushed one of my curls out of my face. "I'm sorry I can't save you from junior high heartache. But I can make some ginger tea. My grandmother said that's the cure for everything."

"Can I have it with honey?" I asked.

"Sure." She hummed as she set a pot on the stove and sliced fresh ginger. Maybe I was feeling mushy because I was tired, but I liked that she told me about her first crush, and that she was making me tea.

I cleared my throat. "Mom? Are you really OK that I like boys?"

Mom stopped humming. "Ezra. Honey." She came back to the island and set her hands on my shoulders. "I try not to pry too much, because I know it's not easy to talk about something so personal when you're thirteen and figuring things out. But I'm more than OK with it. I'm *so* proud of you for having the courage to be who you are."

Suddenly it was dusty in the kitchen. I rubbed my eye under my glasses. "OK, Mom. The water's boiling."

She kissed my cheek and returned to the stove.

I was glad I told her about everything. Now if only ginger tea could prevent the weird dreams from returning.

★★★

The snow piled up so much overnight that school was cancelled the next day. After my late night, I was happy to sleep 'til noon. Late in the afternoon, Brian texted Ty and me.

> Do you guys want to come to the gym before school tomorrow?

Brian had mentioned that Coach Williams opened the gym early for him. This was the first time he'd invited us, though.

> When do you go? Ty wrote back.

Brian: I'm there by 7:15
Ty: Dang that's early. You're hardcore
Me: I'll be there
Ty: Me too
Brian: Cool, thanks

Hopeful thoughts popped into my head: *Maybe he's feeling better if he wants us around. Maybe yesterday really did help.*

I had second thoughts in the morning when my alarm blared forty-five minutes earlier than usual, but I dragged my sleepy butt out of bed and upstairs for a quick breakfast. Dad was drinking coffee and reading the paper, because he was one of those old-fashioned guys who liked to flip through a physical newspaper. He usually muttered about the sad state of journalism while he was at it, and Mom and I smiled. Sometimes it was nice when your parents were predictable.

Dad looked up. "You're up early."

I stifled a yawn. "Yeah, I'm going to the gym with Brian and Ty."

"Really?"

"It's the playoffs, Dad. Gotta be ready."

I scarfed down some toast and a banana and bundled up for the walk. I took my guitar with me, since I had a lesson after school and I was practicing with Madi at lunch. Ty met me on the corner of his street. Even he was quiet this early, so we walked in silence and tried not to wipe out on the snowy sidewalks.

When we got there, Brian was already in the gym, shooting while Coach Williams rebounded. We changed and joined them. I'd noticed in practice, but it was even more obvious this morning: Brian transformed on the court. It was like he was home. I watched the way he concentrated, and I wondered if that was how I looked when

I picked up my guitar. And he'd gotten so *good*, light-years ahead of last year when we were benchwarmers together. He was practically on the same level as Ty now. They moved in sync, reading each other's minds on the court.

Kind of like when I played music with Victor.

When it was time for homeroom, Brian sighed as we put the balls away.

"You'd stay in the gym all day, wouldn't you?" I asked.

"Yeah," he admitted.

I dropped a ball in the storage bin. "I'll come every morning, if you want."

"Me too," Ty added. "This was fun."

"I'd like that," Brian said. "I liked having you guys here."

This was what I could do. I couldn't make Brian better, but I could run drills and rebound for him.

The halls were starting to fill as we left the gym and walked past the music room. The sound of the piano spilled under the door.

Ty paused. "Whoever's playing is really good."

"It's Victor." I said without thinking, and my face heated up. "He hangs out there a lot."

"Huh," Ty said. Brian glanced at me, but he didn't say anything.

"Anyway, uh . . ." I held up my guitar case. "I need to drop this off in there, so I'll catch up with you in class."

I slipped into the music room. Victor heard me and turned around at the piano.

"Oh. Hey." He eyed my guitar case.

"I have a lesson after school," I told him. "And I'm practicing with Madi at lunch. She's going to sing 'Blackbird' for the talent show, so I'm playing for her."

"Nice. You doing your own thing too?"

"Yeah. Still haven't picked a song yet, though."

"You should write one," Victor said. "You already have music. That piece we recorded is great. You just need lyrics."

"Just?" I scoffed. "Like it's that easy."

He gave his half smile. "That's why I stick to instrumentals. But you're good at expressing yourself. I bet you could do it."

Victor met my eyes. He looked like he wanted to say something else, and maybe I did too, but the door swung open and the eighth-grade band class started filing in. Madi, Alicia, Jemma, and Miranda were the first ones through the door. Alicia stopped and said, "Oh," the way someone would say it if they found a rotten banana in their locker.

Victor's face changed instantly. "I should get to class," he mumbled. The girls watched him leave in icy silence.

When he was gone, Madi glanced at my guitar and smiled. "See you at lunch!"

"Yeah, looking forward to it," I told her. I propped my guitar near the piano and headed to class.

All morning, I thought about the things Victor didn't say, and the thing that he did. *"You're good at expressing yourself."*

Could I write an actual song?

I had the music and the melody, but words had always felt like the hardest part. And singing something I'd written myself felt way more terrifying than doing a cover. But the idea wouldn't let me go.

21. THE POWER OF
BUTT JOKES

BRIAN

If I were someone's kid on a TV drama, the "Screaming Shirtless in the Snow" episode would have been my turning point where I vanquished Goblin Mode and everything was fine again. But life didn't work like that. I didn't feel better right away, and things weren't magically cool with Mom after one hug.

I did tell Dr. Bender about how low I felt the night of the snowstorm. She suggested I should talk to my doctor. I did that too, and Dr. Murphy adjusted my medication. And slowly, other things changed. I liked shooting around with Ty and Ezra before school. Ty told Andre about our work-outs, and word spread until the whole team started showing up. Coach mostly watched and let us do our own thing. And it worked, because we won another game, and then another.

The morning before our district final, Ty called everyone into a huddle.

"Guys, we're doing this," he declared. "We're beating Gorsebrook, and then we're winning the regional championship. How much do you want it?"

I was the first to answer. "More than anything."

Everyone looked at me. We didn't talk about it much, but they knew how hard this winter had been for me.

"More than anything," Andre echoed.

Ezra put his hand on my shoulder. "More than anything."

"More than anything," Ty said. "We take down Gorsebrook today, then we work our butts off here tomorrow, and on Saturday we win it all."

We all stuck our hands in the middle of the huddle and yelled, "One—two—three—team!"

The game was in Gorsebrook's gym, but they didn't stand a chance. On the opening tipoff, Ty tapped the ball to me, I spotted Andre streaking to the hoop, and I heaved a pass from half-court into his hands for a layup. Three seconds in, we had our first basket. Our offense flew around at top speed all game, with me in the driver's seat dishing assists as my teammates cut to the rim. When Gorsebrook tried to slow us down with a zone defense, I made them pay by sinking back-to-back three-pointers. I felt like I was in control of the whole court, and it was so much fun that I was almost disappointed when our lead grew so big that Coach pulled the starters with eight minutes left. We watched from the bench as our seventh graders finished off the blowout win.

When the final buzzer sounded, Ty pulled me into a headlock. "We're going to the finals, baby!"

I was so pumped that I didn't even mind being stuck in Ty's sweaty armpit.

He was still bouncing as we headed for his dad's car. "We should celebrate. I'll ask Dad to stop for pizza."

"I thought you said we don't rest until we're champions," I said.

He shrugged. "We can still celebrate along the way. We kicked butt today."

"You keep talking about butts." Ezra put on a sports announcer voice. "Here are today's keys to victory: Work your butt off, kick the other team's butt, and then celebrate. With your butt."

He wiggled his hips, and I laughed.

Ezra stopped. He and Ty stared at me.

"What?" I asked.

Ty was beaming. "That was a real laugh. You haven't done that in forever."

Ezra blinked. "You look different. Kind of . . . happy." He whispered the last word, like he was afraid to say it too loud.

I paused and did an inventory check of my body. I was tired but satisfied after playing so hard. My stomach rumbled; I could go for pizza. Other than that, nothing. No bees in my chest. No voice of doom.

"I feel good," I said. "I *am* happy."

It came out louder than I expected. A bummed-out Gorsebrook player walking past shot me a sour look, like *Good for you, buddy.*

"Is this . . . ?" Ezra couldn't finish his sentence. He was blinking a lot.

"I don't know," I said. "But this is the best I've felt in a long time. Maybe your butt jokes cured me."

Ezra laughed, then he threw his arms around me. I hugged him back tight.

Ty clapped a hand on both of our shoulders. "We should *definitely* get pizza."

"Yeah," I agreed. "I'm starving."

★★★

I was almost afraid to go to sleep at night in case I was riding some temporary wave and I'd feel lousy again tomorrow. But the next morning, I didn't wake up dreading school or dwelling on all the worst things that could happen.

My family had never been religious, but I said "Thanks" out loud as I popped my morning pill and washed it down with orange juice.

Mom breezed into the kitchen. "Who are you talking to?"

"The universe."

"What?"

I turned. "Can Ezra sleep over tonight?"

"Sure, if his parents . . . Wait, you want to have Ezra over?" she asked slowly. I could guess what she was thinking from the way her eyes went wide.

"I'm feeling a little better, Mom. Sorry I've been such a bear lately."

Mom swallowed hard. "It's OK. I . . . Yes. Ezra can come over."

"Thanks. See you this afternoon."

I hurried out before she could get too emotional. On the walk to school, I stuck in my earbuds and cranked some hip-hop, loud. Today, it felt good to be alive.

22. OK ROCK STAR

EZRA

The team was in a great mood at our Friday morning shoot-around. Ty was even more extra than usual, bouncing around the gym and whooping whenever someone made a shot.

"Tomorrow, we win it all," he hollered before we headed to class, and everyone roared in agreement.

Brian was still grinning as we walked to homeroom. "Want to sleep over tonight?" he asked me.

I didn't have the chance to say yes before Ty threw his arms around our shoulders.

"Just don't stay up too late. Tomorrow's the big game. Graham Creighton is tough, but we can take them."

Brian patted Ty's arm. "We promise we'll be good, Mom."

I snickered.

"I'll allow your sarcasm as a sign that you're feeling better," Ty said. "But I'm serious."

"We know," Brian said. "We haven't forgotten your butt speech, Ty. We'll be ready."

"That's the spirit." Ty squeezed our shoulders and let us go.

Brian grinned at me. He looked so happy. I couldn't help grinning back.

A burst of laughter rung out behind us and a pack of boys charged past, sending a herd of seventh graders scrambling out of their way. I recognized two heads in the pack, one blond and one dark-haired.

"Colby!" Ty called.

They stopped. Most of them were ninth graders I only knew from passing in the halls. Colby waved awkwardly.

"Hey, guys." He briefly met my eyes and gave me that irritating little nod before he looked away.

Victor did the same thing.

"Coming to our game tomorrow?" Ty asked. "It's the championship. You'll be there to support your boys, right?" He nodded at the ninth graders. "Me and Colby, we go way back."

The other guys looked from us to Colby.

Colby squirmed. "Uh, yeah. Maybe. We'll see." He was suddenly fascinated by the African Heritage Month poster on Mrs. Clelland's classroom door. "Anyway, see you later."

"Yeah, see you later," Ty said.

"Bye, Colby," I added. He followed his new buds down the hall. When they rounded the corner, I grinned at Ty. "I liked watching Colby sweat a little."

"Doesn't hurt to remind him where he came from." Ty patted my back.

"I like watching Colby sweat too," Brian said. "And I prefer the new quiet version of Victor. It's a massive improvement."

"Maybe he actually learned his lesson from you about running his mouth," Ty cracked.

Now I was the one squirming. But I didn't say anything.

★★★

After school, I headed home to pack for Brian's. I was sliding my basketball jersey into my bag when my phone buzzed with a text. It was from Victor.

Good luck at your game tomorrow

This morning Victor had only given me the *I guess I'll acknowledge that you exist* nod, and now he was texting me good luck?

I guess I couldn't totally blame him. I'd barely acknowledged him either. Not with Brian and Ty watching. Maybe I wasn't any better.

Thanks, I wrote back.

I thought about leaving it at that, then I added, I'm nervous tbh. Playoff games are stressful. Ty takes this VERY seriously

I had instant regret after I sent it, like maybe that was too much. But Victor started typing.

I get it. I always hated hockey playoffs. My dad took them way too seriously

Victor was willingly revealing something about himself? My stomach did a little flip. I didn't know you played, I wrote back.

I don't anymore. How's the songwriting coming?

I guess that was the end of Victor's personal sharing time.

Slowly. Maybe I'll be inspired if we win tomorrow OK Rock Star, he replied. I laughed.

"What's so funny?" Mom asked in my doorway, startling me so bad I jumped. I shoved my phone in my pocket.

"Nothing. And thanks for scaring the crap out of me. You could have knocked."

She rolled her eyes. "So dramatic. Do you want a ride to Brian's?"

"Sure." I finished packing and followed Mom upstairs.

★★★

The finish line was in sight when a Koopa shell smoked me from behind and sent me spinning into a wall. Richie raced past, cackling, with Brian a split second behind him.

Richie threw his arms in the air. "Winner! Again! Eat it, clowns."

"You're both monsters," I moaned.

Brian punched my arm. "The Days show no mercy in *Mario Kart*. Ride or die, baby."

"I'll show you no mercy." I dropped my controller and put them each in a headlock. Brian jabbed his elbow into my thigh, forcing me to let go. Brian's elbows were lethal. We wrestled until we were all cracking up.

A warm buzz shot through me every time Brian laughed.

When we flopped on the couch, Richie peered at me. "Are you growing a mustache?"

I shrugged. "I just haven't shaved yet. It's not that noticeable, is it?"

Brian poked my lip. "It's getting there. Like, one-fifth of a real mustache." He gave me a mischievous grin.

Richie folded his hands behind his head. "I can't wait to grow one. I'm going to look so hot with a mustache."

"Yeah, good luck with that, Rich," Brian snickered.

I stroked my upper lip. "Maybe I *should* grow one. It could add to my rock star aura."

"Did you find a bass player for your band?" Richie asked.

Brian gave me a sideways look. "Since when do you have a band?"

"I don't. I was just joking with Richie."

"Oh." He looked at me for a second longer, and I wasn't sure what he was thinking. Then he hopped up to get snacks.

We abandoned *Mario Kart* and watched a movie before calling it a night. We texted Ty to assure him we were going to bed. When the light was out, Brian rolled toward me.

"Thanks for coming over. This was fun. I know I haven't been very fun lately."

"I had fun too," I told him. "And don't apologize for—"

"I know." He went quiet. "I feel like I missed a lot, though. Like, what's new with you? The talent show's coming up, right? What are you going to play?"

"I haven't totally decided yet, but . . ." I exhaled. "I'm kind of maybe writing a song."

"Really?" Brian propped up on one elbow. "That's great! Can I hear it sometime? If you're giving sneak previews."

I thought about telling him how making music with Victor had sparked all kinds of creative ideas, and how I didn't know what to do with the Victor Dilemma. But tonight had been great, and he was just starting to feel better. I didn't want to ruin the vibe.

"Maybe, if I finish it," I said.

"Whatever you play, I know it will be great. You're a rock star, Ezra."

He yawned, and we drifted off to sleep.

23. SUPERVILLAINS

BRIAN

The Capital Region championship took place at Citadel High, where Gabe and Brittany went to school. They brought a bunch of their friends and filled up half a row of the packed bleachers, and Gabe hopped down during warm-ups to give us fist bumps.

He massaged my shoulders. "You got this, Brian. Go win a championship."

Mom was there too, and Richie, and Mrs. Clelland, along with a few other teachers from school. Ms. Virth was banging a cowbell, which was both embarrassing and hilarious.

I wished Dad could be here.

I made Kevan promise to record some videos that I could share with Dad later. I was surprised how many other kids from school were there on a Saturday. Madi Jacobs called Ezra's name and waved. It had been a while since Halifax North played for a banner, so I guess some school spirit had kicked in.

Ty glanced toward the far end of the gym. "Well, look at that. I didn't think Colby and Victor would actually show up."

Ezra turned to stare. "Huh."

The clock ticked toward tipoff. Graham Creighton Junior High was big and strong, and they had a kid named Demar Downey who was one of the best scorers around. Ty played with him on the provincial team, and they were friends when they weren't facing each other for a championship.

"I'm coming for you, Ty," Demar yelled as we finished warm-ups.

"I'm ready," Ty hollered back. He bounced on his toes. "Let's do this."

I felt my usual pregame jitters—the ARPs had hit hard and I'd gone to the bathroom four times already—but I was excited too. I knew we could do this. The universe owed me.

Apparently, the universe disagreed.

Demar didn't miss once in the opening minutes, and he rocketed Creighton to a 10–2 lead. Ty picked up two quick fouls trying to stop him, and Coach had to take him out for a while, since you only got five fouls in a game and we couldn't afford to lose Ty too early. He slapped the bench in frustration as Harrison replaced him.

Just as we started to settle down and find a rhythm, Andre collided with a Creighton defender midair as they battled for a rebound, and when he landed, his knee buckled. He fell to the floor and screamed. The gym went silent, except for Andre moaning.

We huddled by our bench, shell-shocked. Coach and Andre's dad helped him to the bench. As they approached, we could tell it was bad.

"We should take you to the hospital," his dad said.

Andre grimaced. "I have to stay. For the team."

His dad shook his head. "There's no way you can play."

"I *know*." Andre's voice cracked. "But I'm not leaving."

He sat at the end of the bench, gritting his teeth. We were seven minutes into the game, our two top scorers were out, and one wasn't coming back. This was a disaster. I put my hands on my head and took deep breaths to try to cut off the growing tightness in my chest.

"Hang in there, guys," Coach Williams said. "Stay focused."

We tried. I switched to guarding Demar and did a decent job slowing him down, but we were still cold on offense. Jayden couldn't make a shot, and Harrison was—well, he wasn't Ty.

My frustration spiked as I fought through Creighton's swarming defense and found open teammates, only to watch their shots clank off the rim. I cursed under my breath as Harrison rushed a putback attempt and missed from three feet.

When the buzzer sounded for halftime, we were down 36–21. We retreated to the locker room, with Andre hopping on one leg as he held on to Jayden and Harrison for support.

It was as quiet as a funeral. My chest buzzed, and ugly thoughts crowded my mind. I tried to shake them off. I wanted to be done with Goblin Mode. I didn't want to go back there.

"So, that wasn't great," Coach said.

"No kidding," Jayden sighed. He glanced at Andre. "We're missing you bad, man."

Andre's eyes clouded. It hit me that this was the last junior high game for him and all our ninth graders. It wasn't fair that after everything, he had to watch from the bench.

"You guys can't go out like chumps," he said. "We can still beat these guys."

"That's right," Ty insisted. "It's not over."

"It's not even close to over," Coach said. "We'll have more minutes from Ty in the second half. Be smart out there, Ty. No more fouls. Ezra, you're starting the second half. And Brian, you're helping us stay in this game, but we need you to shoot more. Run the pick and roll with Ty, and when you're open, let it fly."

"For real." Andre gave me a determined look. "You're one of our best shooters. Light it up."

The whole team looked at me like they were counting on me. I nodded tightly. "Got it."

We mustered as much enthusiasm as we could for a cheer. As everyone was leaving the locker room, Ty and Ezra stopped me.

"You OK?" Ezra asked.

I was tempted to say "Yeah" and keep going. But I didn't want to pretend with my friends anymore.

"No," I admitted. "I'm starting to feel Goblin-y."

"Good," Ty said. "Use it."

Ezra and I looked at him in surprise.

"Don't get me wrong, don't start a fight or anything," Ty added. "But just let it out, B. It's OK to be mad. I'm mad too."

I glanced at Ezra. He let out a breath. "Maybe Ty's right. Maybe you hold things in too much." He grinned. "Be spicy, Spicy B."

Maybe they were both right.

"I want to win this game so bad it hurts," I said.

"That's what I'm talking about." Ty poked my chest. "It's time for us to become supervillains."

The locker room door swung open. "Everything OK in here?" Coach Williams asked.

"We're good, Coach," Ty answered. "Just talking about how we're taking over this game."

"Great." Coach gave me a fist bump. "Keep shooting."

On our first play of the second half, Ty screened my defender and I launched a three-pointer. *Swish.*

After Creighton missed, we ran the same play and this time I threaded a pass to Ty when his man rushed out to stop me from shooting. Ty made a layup, and the lead was down to ten.

"Let's go!" I yelled.

The rest of the third quarter was the Brian and Ty Super-villain Attack. After all those early mornings together, we could find each other without even thinking. If Ty screened for me, I pulled up and shot or lobbed him a no-look pass for a layup. Sometimes we flipped roles and Ty found me for an open shot or drove to the hoop if the defense was slow to react. When Creighton switched to a zone, I drove at the hoop and whipped the ball to Ezra, who was open in the corner when the defense collapsed on me. Ezra drained his shot and pumped his fist. The buzzer sounded to end the quarter, and suddenly we were only down by two points.

"Yes!" I hollered. I'd never been this loud on the court before, but it felt right. The buzz in my chest had turned into electricity—I'd played almost the whole game and I was still energized for the fourth quarter. Maybe Ty was onto something.

But Creighton wasn't giving up. Demar started the quarter with a three-pointer to push their lead to five, and we seesawed back and forth. Every time we got close, they found a way to answer. After Demar stole the ball from Jayden and raced downcourt for a layup, their lead was back to 68–62 with only fifteen seconds to play. The Creighton players high-fived and their fans went wild.

Coach called timeout and we headed to the bench. Jayden hung his head.

"It's not over," I reminded him. Six points was a lot to make up in fifteen seconds, but we couldn't give up yet. I wanted this game so bad.

Coach drew a play for me to shoot a quick three. When the play started, I wove through my teammates and caught Ty's inbound pass high above the three-point line. Demar raced at me, but his momentum was carrying him forward too quickly to adjust. I faked left, dribbled hard to the right, and launched.

Swish. 68–65. Our fans went bananas.

Eleven seconds left.

Creighton inbounded right away instead of calling timeout, hoping to catch us off guard before we set up our defense. But Ty knocked their pass away, and Ezra grabbed the ball and hurled it to me behind the three-point line. I caught and launched in one motion, barely clearing Demar's outstretched fingertips. He crashed into me on his way down. The referee blew his whistle, signaling a foul while the ball was in the air. I tumbled to the court with Demar.

Then the gym erupted as the ball dropped through the net.

Tie game, 68–68 with two seconds left. And I had a free throw for a chance to give us the lead.

Ty and Ezra scooped me off the floor. Ty was so wired he was almost vibrating. Ezra's eyes were wide behind his sports glasses. They walked me to the free-throw line, and everyone lined up.

Hundreds of eyes were on me. This could be the shot that decided the championship game.

I didn't look at anyone. I did what I did every time I took a free throw: three dribbles, spun the ball in my hands, stared at the rim, exhaled, and shot.

Swish.

We were ahead by one.

Creighton called timeout, and I glanced at the stands as I walked toward the bench. Gabe was pointing at me and screaming with a huge grin on his face. Kevan was yelling too, and Richie was hopping up and down, and Mom was wiping her eyes. Basically everyone was cheering for me.

"You scored seven points in thirteen seconds!" Ty hollered in my ear. "That's the most badass thing I've ever seen!"

My teammates whooped, and even Harrison slapped me on the back. Coach signaled for quiet. Then a smile slipped out.

"That really was badass." Everyone hollered some more. He held up his hand again.

"Two seconds," he said. "Two seconds to play the best defense of your life. Don't give up any easy shots, and whatever you do, don't foul." He looked at me. "You know they want the ball in Demar's hands."

I nodded. "I won't let him score."

I went to Demar immediately as Creighton walked back on the court. He lined up with his teammates. The referee handed the ball to the inbounding player and started counting. They had five seconds to inbound, then the clock started.

I chased Demar through two screens, keeping a hand in his face. I didn't want him catching the ball, and if he did, I wanted him off-balance, so he couldn't get a clean shot. I did my job perfectly. I saw the desperation in his eyes as he bobbed and weaved, trying to get open. But I wouldn't let him go.

As the inbounder was running out of time, he turned away from Demar, but he found one of his teammates near the baseline and threw a pass.

I was stuck to Demar, too far away to get to the ball. Jayden was a step late as the Creighton player collected the pass and shot. The buzzer sounded while the ball was in the air, and a split second later, it kissed off the backboard and dropped through the net.

Game over. Graham Creighton won, 70–69.

Demar screamed in celebration and dove into a pile with his teammates. Creighton fans poured onto the court. I stood with my hands on my head, numb.

I couldn't believe it. After all that energy, all that sweat, all the shots I made to lead a huge comeback, we still lost.

We lost.

I fell to my knees and burst into tears.

I hated that I was crying on the floor in a packed gym, but I couldn't help it. I'd tried *so hard*. All I'd done for months was try. Every single day.

I was sobbing so hard my shoulders shook.

Ty wrapped his arms around me. He was crying too. "This sucks, B. We were so close."

Ezra joined us and we sat there, blubbering. When we finally stood up, the whole team was around us, everyone sniffling and wiping their faces on their jerseys. Andre's eyes were red as he leaned on Jayden.

Even Coach was misty. He clapped a hand on my shoulder. "I don't even know how to tell you how proud I am," he said, his voice raspy. "You played your heart out, and they just hit one more shot today. That's how it goes sometimes. But you played like a champion, Brian. You were a real leader."

My throat was still lumpy, and I swallowed hard.

Eventually, we lined up to shake hands with the Creighton players. It hurt to see them celebrating, knowing how close we'd come to being in their shoes, but I couldn't be mad at them.

Demar gave me a shoulder bump. "No one's played me that tough all year," he said. "You should try out for the provincial team with me and Ty."

"Thanks," I said. It felt good to get a compliment from a player as good as Demar. It felt even better when Gabe and his high-school buddies surrounded me.

"Brian, you were *clutch*." Gabe punched my chest. "You hit seven threes! You scored thirty-two points, and I bet you had a triple-double." He grinned. "You were fired up too. I love seeing you like that."

"That was unreal," added a huge kid with a deep voice. "Those last two threes were daggers, man. You got one enormous set of—"

"Ahem." Mrs. Clelland stepped into the circle. The guy didn't finish his sentence, and his friends snickered.

She smiled at me. "I've watched more games than I can count, and your second half today was maybe the best performance I've ever seen."

Gabe covered his heart. "Mom, *ouch*. Better than the time I hung forty on Cole Harbour?"

Mrs. Clelland shrugged. "The stakes were higher."

Gabe's friends laughed. "She's got you there," another razzed him.

Brittany gave me a hug. Richie and Kevan rushed over and re-enacted my game-tying three-pointer, with Kevan falling on Richie like Demar landed on me. Then the moms descended on us—mine, Ty's, and Ezra's—and decided they needed a group picture. We protested, but no kids had ever won an argument with three moms who wanted a photo. We stood against the wall with Ty in the middle, his arms around our shoulders.

"I love you guys," Ty said as our moms snapped away. "And next year we're winning it all. Sizzle Squad domination."

"Deal," I said. "Next year is ours."

The sting of losing faded a little as Mrs. Clelland drove me, Mom, and Richie home. I was still haunted by those last two seconds, but I thought about what Ty said. I'd proven I could play against anyone. Ty and I were practically unstoppable when we got on a roll, and Ezra had hit some big shots too. We'd keep working all spring and summer, and next year, we'd finish junior high as champions.

I leaned against the headrest. It had been a while since thinking about the future felt exciting instead of exhausting. Something had been different on the court today too. Ty was right about playing with emotion—but I guess Gabe had been telling me the same things, and Dr. Bender too, in her own way. I got so swept up in the game that I'd stopped wrestling with the goblin and just played. I'd felt confident. It had felt *good*.

Now if only I could figure out how to do that outside the basketball court.

24. THE SWEATY UNDERWEAR EXCUSE

EZRA

As we were leaving Citadel High, Mom ran down a checklist.

"You've got your sport glasses, right?"

"Yeah, in my backpack."

"Sneakers?"

"Mom."

"What? Like you've never left a pair behind."

"I was *nine*."

"What about your water bottle?"

"Uh—" I unzipped my backpack. It wasn't there. Mom shot me a *See?* look. "Meet you at the car," I grumbled, and headed back inside.

The gym was nearly empty by the time I found my bottle in a corner of the gym. I looked over the court and a pang tugged at my chest. I liked basketball. Today had been the most incredible game I'd ever played in, and I loved watching Brian unlock superstar mode. He and Ty were amazing, and it felt great to be part of it. But I didn't live for basketball like they did. I was sure they'd spend the rest of the day thinking ahead to next season, but I was already testing out new song lyrics in my head.

As I left the gym, I saw Victor and Madi in the hall, arguing.

"Forget it, Victor. It's too late!" Madi said, then she stormed out the door.

Victor turned chili-pepper red the way he'd done in Ms. Floriman's office, and he squeezed his fists like he was trying not to explode. Then he slumped against the wall.

I approached slowly so I didn't startle him. "Victor? You OK?"

His eyes were shut, and he didn't open them until he took a few deep breaths and the color in his face started to fade.

"I'm fine." His voice was tight. "I was just asking Madi about Alicia. It didn't go well."

"Yeah, I saw . . . Are you, uh, trying to get back together with her?"

Victor shook his head. "No chance of that. I'd kind of like it if she didn't hate me, but it might be too late for that too." He looked away. "Anyway, good game today. Sorry how it ended. I know how much it sucks to lose on the last shot."

I tried not to focus on the helplessness I'd felt as Graham Creighton's buzzer-beater dropped through the net. Or the weird tingle of relief that just hit me when Victor said he wasn't trying to get back with Alicia.

"Yeah. That was rough." I looked around. "Where's Colby? Wasn't he with you?"

"He had to go."

I rolled my eyes. "Of course."

"Still mad at him, huh?" Victor tilted his head. "What do you want from Colby, anyway?"

What do I want? Why does everyone keep asking me that?

"It *hurt*, Victor," I said. "Colby was my friend for a long time. It seems like you can just shake things off—or maybe you only act that way—but Colby moved on like nothing ever happened, and that didn't feel good. And I don't know how to just get over that."

My face prickled. I hadn't meant to blurt all that out. I half expected Victor to defend Colby or tell me I was over-reacting, but he stared at the floor.

"I guess that's fair," he said.

"Yeah. Anyway, my mom's waiting." I started toward the door.

Victor followed. "Want to come over?"

This caught me off guard. Part of me wanted to go, but it was still so complicated. There was the Victor when it was just us, and the Victor when he was with Colby and their friends. Then there was the shadow of the Victor who'd hurt my friends last year. And on top of all that, I still couldn't figure out how current Victor felt about me, or how I *wanted* to feel about him. It was one big knot I didn't have the energy to untangle right now.

"I'm pretty tired," I said. "And sweaty. Maybe another time?"

If Victor was offended, he didn't show it. He was back to inscrutable mode. "OK. You don't smell that bad, though. I could live with it." He gave me his half grin.

"It's not your nose I'm worried about. You know when you cool down after sweating and the waistband of your underwear goes soggy and disgusting? That's kind of where I'm at."

I instantly regretted this TMI overload, but Victor laughed. Like, a real laugh. I wasn't expecting the way it made my heart flutter.

"Understood. Sweaty underwear chafing is no joke. Go deal with . . . all that." He waved in the direction of my underwear, which made my cheeks heat up. "Text you later."

He gave me a mock salute, and we split up.

Mom looked up from her phone as I climbed in the passenger seat. "I was starting to think you'd lost it."

For a second I had no idea what she was talking about until I remembered the water bottle in my hand.

"Uh, yeah. Someone moved it, I guess."

As we pulled out of the parking lot, I watched Victor cross the Common, alone.

25. HOPE AND HOT SAUCE

BRIAN

My face tingled and my breathing was tight as we entered the correctional center. We were all here today—Mom, Richie, and me—for the first time since Christmas.

When I'd told Mom I wanted to go today, Richie said he'd come too. Mom and I were shocked. But I caught the way Richie looked at me, and I knew he was coming for me.

Nobody talked as we waited. I could tell Richie was nervous too, and my big-brother instincts kicked in. I silently challenged him to a thumb war. He grinned, and we were hunched over the table trying to pin each other's thumbs when the door opened.

Dad's eyes went misty when he saw us. He cleared his throat. He was probably trying to think of something clever to say, so he sounded calm. But before he could speak, I hugged him. I couldn't find words either, so I hoped my hug said it all: *I missed you. I'm sorry. I love you.*

He squeezed me back. Mom joined us. Then Richie. And I didn't care that I was crying in jail the day after I'd cried in a school gym.

After we wiped our eyes, we sat and Dad mustered a smile. "Tell me about the game."

"Dad, it was amazing!" Richie jumped in. He was so animated that I sat back and let him tell the story. It was fun listening to my little brother describe my heroics. When he finished, I showed Dad the videos Kevan had taken. Dad's eyes bulged when he saw my back-to-back threes in the final fifteen seconds.

"B-Man, holy—" Dad cursed, earning a mortified *"Everett!"* from Mom. Dad tapped my shoulder. "I wish I could have seen you play this year. You're a serious baller, kiddo."

"I'm thinking about trying out for the provincial summer team with Ty," I said. "Tryouts are in a few weeks."

Mom's head tilted. I hadn't mentioned this to her yet.

Dad's eyes lit up "Definitely! Good for you."

"If I made it, there'd be a lot of weekend practices and travel and stuff. I know that's tricky for us, but Ty said I could get rides with him, if I need."

"Go for it, Brian. Don't worry about that. And besides . . ." He paused and looked at Mom. She inhaled and gave him a tight nod.

My face tingled. "What?"

Dad grinned. "I'll be out on remission by mid-April."

I blinked. "You mean . . . *out* out? Home?"

"Yeah." Dad beamed. I glanced at Mom. Her eyes were shining, but she smiled.

Richie jumped up and hugged Dad again. I followed, waiting for it all to sink in as I was pressed to his shoulder. I'd known—I'd hoped—he might get out early. Corrections and sentencing were topics I'd googled a lot, and I'd learned that Dad could have up to a third of his sentence reduced for good behavior. But suddenly that wasn't abstract anymore. Mid-April was six weeks away. It was a lot closer than July.

Our time ended too soon, as always. But the ache of leaving wasn't as bad today. Richie practically bounced down the hall, which was the first time I'd ever seen him do that here. Mom set a hand on my back.

We weren't natural optimists, Mom and me. We usually defaulted to the worst-case scenario. I understood why she hadn't mentioned anything about Dad's release before today. She'd waited until she was sure, to protect us from disappointment. Maybe to protect herself too. But I saw a glint of hope in her eyes now.

I knew life wasn't always fair. There wasn't a cosmic score sheet where everything evened out if you were nice enough or adopted enough kittens or whatever. But I wanted to believe we deserved a break. Maybe that was what hope was: knowing how the world had always worked and still believing things could get better anyway.

★★★

In March, the light lasted a little longer every day, and I remembered that winter would eventually end. Not every day was great, but the Green Goblin was quieter. Even though basketball season had ended, Coach still opened the gym early, and I shot with Ty and some of the guys before school. Ezra showed up less often now that he was focused on the talent show coming up after March Break. He spent a lot of lunch periods and afternoons practicing with Madi or working on his own song.

On Friday night at the end of March Break, Ty, Kevan, and I slept over at Ezra's. It was the first time all four of us had done that in months. And we were ready to make it epic.

We each hunched over a plate of hot wings in Ezra's kitchen. Kevan raised an eyebrow at me.

"You sure you're ready for this heat? I know you're at a disadvantage because of your unseasoned European genes. If you want to drop out, I understand."

"Please," I scoffed. "You're just playing mind games because you're scared. They don't call me Spicy B for nothing."

"Ooh, B is ready to fight," Ty cackled. "Let's do this."

The rules were simple: First to eat ten wings won. They were coated in Kevan's homemade sauce, and he'd warned us it was fatality-level spicy.

I was ready.

"On three," Ezra said. "One—"

Everyone picked up a wing.

"Two—"

You're going down, Kevan mouthed.

"Three!"

We dove in. Kevan wasn't joking: If the wrong person bit into these wings, their face would melt like the Nazis at the end of *Raiders of the Lost Ark.* I was sweating by the second wing. But it felt amazing. I might have been the palest guy at the table, but I loved spicy food.

Ty was the first to break. He was inhaling his seventh wing when he started coughing. He guzzled a can of root beer—then coughed mid-swallow and pop sprayed out of his nose. Tears streamed down his cheeks as he frantically fanned his face. Ezra cracked up laughing, and then he was coughing too.

I locked eyes with Kevan. We both tore into our last wing, dropped the bones on our plates, and shouted "Done!" at the same time.

"It's a tie," Ty croaked as he wiped his eyes with his sleeve.

Kevan scowled. "A *tie?*"

I scooped an uneaten wing off Ty's plate and stuffed the whole thing in my mouth. Five seconds later, I pulled out the bone and thumped my chest. "I win!"

Kevan slapped the table. "What? That doesn't count!"

Ty and Ezra were both losing it. I threw my arms in the air. "Winner!"

"No way," Kevan insisted. "I refuse to accept defeat against a cheating white guy. This is a hate crime!"

I launched into a victory dance, shaking my hips and flapping my arms like a chicken. Ezra was slumped over the table laughing and Ty could barely catch his breath.

"Brian, you are *neon pink*," Ty gasped. "I didn't know anyone could turn that color."

Even Kevan finally broke. "OK, fine, you can have this one if you'll stop doing *that*."

I gave him one last wiggle for good measure. Ezra grinned at me. It had been a long time since we'd laughed this much together.

"Those were the best wings ever," I told Kevan. "I might pay for them later, though."

"Thanks," Kevan said. "But if you get the runs, it's because your body knows you cheated."

Ty shook his head. "Let it go, Kev."

After we cleaned up, we headed to the basement and turned on the Raptors game. We were half watching, and mostly just talking, when Ezra's phone rang.

Kevan yawned. "Who's calling you so late?"

Ezra's eyebrows furrowed as he checked. Then he hopped up and disappeared into his room to take the call.

26. WORLD-COLLIDING CHAOS

EZRA

Colby. Colby hadn't said more than *Hey* to me in nine months, and now he was calling on a Friday night. That was weird enough, but when I answered, he was breathing hard, like he'd been running.

"Ezra. Hey. I know this is random, but can we come over?" He let out a shaky breath. "It's kind of an emergency."

I had a ton of questions, but I started with the most immediate one. "Where are you?"

"Um . . . almost to your front door."

"Oh. OK. Just a second."

I hung up, blurted a quick "Be right back" to my friends, and headed upstairs. Colby had said *we*, and I was 99 percent sure Victor was with him. I wasn't ready for the world-colliding chaos of Victor and Brian in my house at the same time. I needed to think of a nice way to tell Colby it wasn't a good time. But then I opened the door, and all that disappeared.

It was pouring rain. Colby wore a jacket with the hood up, but Victor was only wearing a sweatshirt. He was soaked through, hair plastered to his head. But what really stood out was his bruised eye and the gash across his swollen cheek.

"Oh my gosh," I blurted. "Come in."

Colby barely met my eyes, but I could worry about him later. Victor winced as he slipped off his shoes.

"What happened?" I reached for his shoulder, then pulled back when I got a whiff of barf.

Before he could answer, Mom came down from the second floor. "Ezra, who's at the door?" She gasped when she saw Victor's face.

"It's not as bad as it looks," he offered in his usual even tone, but Mom still fussed as she ushered him into the kitchen.

Naturally, everyone in the basement came to see what was happening, and suddenly there were seven of us around the kitchen island.

"Colby?" Ty exclaimed.

Kevan stared at Victor and whistled. "You look rough. You tick off the wrong guy and get punched in the face again?" He grinned at Brian standing beside him.

"Kevan, come *on*," I groaned.

Brian didn't say anything. I couldn't tell if he was feeling anxious. I gave him my best *I'm sorry, this just happened* look.

Mom took charge. She positioned Victor so she could examine his face in the light. "Are you dizzy? Nauseous? Any blurred vision?"

"I don't have a concussion, Mrs. Komizarek," he said.

"It's *Ms. Lewis*," Kevan corrected. "Ezra's mom goes by her own name. She's a lawyer."

"Jeez, Kevan, you have no chill," Colby muttered.

A year ago, it would have sounded like a joke, and we would have all laughed. But everything was different now.

"Leave Kevan alone," Ty snapped.

Colby's face darkened. This was already going as badly as I'd feared. I glanced at Brian again. He'd taken a step back, like he was thinking about bailing.

"What happened?" I asked, before everything fell apart.

Victor nodded at Colby. Colby swallowed and studied his hands. He was usually so sure of himself. But right now, he looked scared.

"You two have a seat," Mom said gently, guiding Colby and Victor onto stools. "Paul," she called upstairs to Dad, "bring the first aid kit from the hall closet, please."

Nobody said anything until Dad came downstairs in plaid pajama pants and a faded T-shirt with *Atlantic Ortho-dontist Classic* across the chest, some freebie from a work golf tournament.

"Why do you need . . . oh." Dad gave Victor a curious look as he set the kit on the counter. Mom opened it and started dabbing Victor's face with an antiseptic wipe. He winced but didn't protest.

"All right, Colby," Mom said. "What happened?"

Colby let out a shuddery breath. "We were at my place. Mom and Dad are away—"

Mom's eyebrow raised. My parents were pretty laid-back, but they wouldn't let me have a sleepover with no adults around. Colby dodged Mom's look.

"Jackson decided to have a bunch of people over," he continued. "He knew he wasn't allowed, but . . . anyway. Victor's brother Wilbur came, and a few other guys, and some girls, and they were drinking. We mostly stayed in my room. But, um . . ."

He glanced at Victor and bit his lip. "We heard Jackson and Wilbur going to Jackson's room, and they had a girl with them, but she was totally out of it. She could barely walk." Colby's voice went raspy. "It felt wrong."

Mom drew a sharp breath. I felt cold all over.

"Colby, what happened?" The urgency in Mom's tone made my heart race.

Colby sat up straighter. "Victor stopped them. He blocked Jackson's door and wouldn't let them in. Then Wilbur attacked him."

Everyone looked at Victor. He was still wearing his usual calm expression, even with his banged-up face. I watched my friends as their images of him began to shift. He'd done some awful stuff last year, but he'd risked getting beat up to protect a girl he didn't know. There was more to him than his worst moments.

I glanced at Colby, and my stomach twinged. He had his own flaws, but he'd seen the better parts of Victor before I had.

"This girl, is she safe?" Mom asked.

"Yeah," Victor said. "Colby got Wilbur off me by kicking him right where it hurts. Wilbur was so messed up, he puked on me. When Jackson came at him, Colby kicked him too. We left them both moaning on the floor."

Colby shrugged. "They deserved it."

"Another girl came upstairs to see what was happening, and she started yelling at Jackson and Wilbur," Victor continued. "She got her friend out of there, and we told everyone Colby's parents were coming and made sure they called a ride. Then we left before Jackson and Wilbur could come after us."

"Did you actually call your parents?" Mom asked.

Colby shook his head.

Mom pursed her lips. "Well, you did the right thing getting everyone to leave, but your parents need to know what happened. I'll call them."

Colby's face fell. "Do you have to? Jackson's going to kill me."

"I do," Mom said firmly. "And you shouldn't have to worry about Jackson."

"This is so messed up." Colby buried his face in his hands. His shoulders shook as he started crying.

Victor put a hand on his back. "It's all right, Co."

I was in shock as Colby cried and Victor comforted him. I wanted to do something, anything, but I was frozen.

Ty moved first. "It's messed up, but you guys did good." He patted Colby's shoulder and gave Victor a little nod.

"And you kicked Jackson in the junk!" Kevan added.

Colby snort-laughed through his sniffles. "Yeah, I've been wanting to do that forever."

I still didn't know what to do. Brian had slid closer to my side, and I wondered what he was thinking. We'd been having such a perfect night. Now everything had changed.

Mom turned to Victor. "We should call your parents too. They might want to get you checked out."

For the first time, Victor's expression faltered. "I'm OK, honest. This isn't the worst Wilbur's ever done to me. And my mom's not home. It's her first weekend away in forever and I don't want to ruin it."

"And your father?" Mom asked slowly, like she'd already guessed it was a sensitive topic.

Victor scowled. "Dad and I don't get along. I'm supposed to be at his place this weekend. That's why I went to Colby's. Honestly, he'll probably take Wilbur's side."

The room went quiet again.

"Dude," Kevan said heavily.

Mom exhaled. "Well, I'm calling your mom, Colby, but you can both stay here while we sort this out."

Colby turned to me. It was the first time we'd made eye contact since he showed up.

I finally found my voice. "Of course you can stay. I'm glad you came."

"Thank you," Colby whispered. "I knew I could count on you."

I bit my lip.

"I'm going to make ginger tea," Mom announced. "That'll warm you up and calm you down. But Victor, we have to get you out of those wet clothes. You're shivering!"

"I'll lend you some clothes." It came out more quickly than I intended, and my face went hot. "Come on, Victor," I mumbled. He followed me downstairs.

★★★

"Sorry I smell like Wilbur's puke," Victor said. "Most of it washed off in the rain, but I still stink." He descended the stairs slowly, and his breath hitched on every second step. I could tell he was in pain.

"What you did was really brave," I told him.

He shrugged. "I did what had to be done. You would've done the same."

I wanted to believe he was right. But I also didn't want to think about being in that situation.

I led him to my bathroom and found him a towel. "You can take a shower to warm up and rinse off the barf. I'll get you some clothes."

"Thanks."

I started to leave as he tried to slip off his sweatshirt, but I wasn't even to the door when he swore softly. He had his right arm out of his shirt, and his face was screwed up in agony.

"So . . . I can't lift my left arm very far. I'm kind of stuck."

I took a step closer. "Do you need help?"

"Yeah."

I carefully lifted his collar over his head and slid the sleeve down his arm. I couldn't help wincing. Victor's left side was covered in darkening splotches. He was still playing it cool, but I knew he was hurting. I wanted to give him a hug, but he might hate that, and it would probably be weird, and it wouldn't help his bruised ribs.

"Do you, uh, need anything else?" I asked.

He glanced down at his jeans. "I think I can handle the rest."

"Sure. I'll go get you some clothes then." My face nearly burst into flames, and I hurried back to my room. As I was gathering an outfit for Victor, I heard the others up in the kitchen. Muffled voices, then Kevan and Colby laughing. It was familiar and strange all at once.

I wondered how Brian was doing. It had to be weird for him. Colby wasn't very nice to him either last year.

This wasn't how I'd expected tonight to go at all.

The shower was still running, so I left a pile of clothes on the bathroom counter—boxers, sweatpants, a tank top, and a zip-up hoodie. Then I waited outside in case Victor needs anything.

"Ezra?" he called two minutes later. "You can come in."

I opened the door. He had just my sweatpants on, and he held out the tank top. "Don't want to get stuck again."

I tried not to stare at his bruised chest as I helped him slip the tank top around his arms and over his head. "I thought it might be easier than a T-shirt, but I guess not. I'm glad everything fits, though. Especially, uh, my boxers. I wasn't sure."

Victor raised an eyebrow. "Are you saying I have a big butt?"

"I'd say your butt is the proper size," I shot back, and Victor grinned—a full smile, not his usual half grin. My stomach fluttered.

I offered him the hoodie, but he shook his head. "I'm all right, thanks."

"Do you want an ice pack for your ribs, or Tylenol or something? I can ask Mom—"

"I'm good, Ezra."

We were still standing really close together. Neither of us moved.

I cleared my throat. "Can I ask a weird question?"

"Sure."

"You didn't fight back, did you?"

The flicker in his eyes told me that wasn't the weird question he was expecting. "I told you, I don't fight. Not even Wilbur. He's always trying to get me to, but I won't give him the satisfaction." An edge crept into his voice. "I don't want to be like him."

"Oh." My glasses were fogging up from the shower steam, and I wiped them on the hem of my shirt. "Is that why you didn't do anything when I tackled you in the hall?"

"That was different."

"What do you mean?"

"I knew you weren't trying to hurt me. You were protecting Brian. And the way you came flying in like that, all fierce . . ." Victor's half grin returned. "It was kind of hot."

My whole face tingled. I took a step back. "Are you messing with me?"

"What? No!" Victor's eyes went wider than I'd ever seen them. "Ezra, I . . . You know I have a crush on you, right? I've been dropping hints forever."

I froze. Suddenly I was hyperaware of everything—the sound of the bathroom fan, the moisture dripping on the mirror, the smell of my body wash coming from Victor. The whole room seemed more vivid now that I knew this one world-changing detail.

"Well, why didn't you just *say* that?" I blurted out, which wasn't the smoothest response, but it had been a weird night. "Of course I didn't know. I mean, I thought *maybe*, but I can never tell what you're thinking. Honestly, you're impossible sometimes! And I think you like it that way. Plus, you dated Alicia, and I figured you could be bi, but I didn't want to assume—"

"Ezra." Victor mercifully stopped me. "I really liked Alicia, even though I messed that up. But . . . I like you now. A lot." His cheeks were turning pink. "I know I can be—"

"Mysterious? Inscrutable?"

"It's a control thing. Dr. Wright helped me figure that out." Victor sighed. "I asked him how I'm supposed to, like, *talk* to you, and he said I should be honest. But Colby had said that too, so I guess I didn't need to hear it from a psychologist."

I blinked. "You told *Colby*?"

"No, he figured it out from how I talk about you. But he's cool with it." Victor looked me in the eye. "I told you, he's changing too."

For a moment, I pictured Colby upstairs with the others. But before I got too far down that road, Victor took a deep breath.

"So, I'll be honest. I've never felt this way about another guy before, and I didn't know what to do with that at first, but I like you a lot. I love watching you play guitar, and I like being around you, and, uh . . ."

He was *nervous*. I'd never seen him like this, and it made me all tingly.

He bit his lip. "I've been afraid to tell you, because you're a great guy, and you deserve someone better than me. My record's not great." He smiled weakly. "Really sold myself there, huh?"

"Victor." I inched closer. "Honestly, trying to figure you out is a lot. And we still have stuff we should talk about. But . . . I like you too."

"Really?" Victor's face lit up in a full smile, and it made the tingles grow stronger.

"Really."

We drifted closer, and the air felt thick, and my hand was on his shoulder, and my heart was thumping, and Victor leaned in—

"Ezra? Victor?" Brian called. I jumped like I'd touched a live wire.

"We're here! We're good!" I answered, way too loudly. Victor deflated a little.

Brian appeared in the doorway. He was holding a steaming mug in one hand and an ice pack in the other. "I have tea, and you're supposed to put this on your face, Victor. The ice, not the tea." He looked at me. "Everything all right?"

"Yeah, of course! I, uh, I mean we—" *Why was I still shouting?*

"I needed a hand," Victor said. He gingerly lifted his shirt and showed Brian his bruises.

Brian gaped. "Oh. *Ouch.* Well, I'll just . . ." He placed the tea and the ice pack on the counter and backed away.

"It's OK, we're finished." My words still came too fast and loud. I didn't look back at Victor. I hoped he wasn't disappointed. But we couldn't just go back to . . . whatever we were about to do. The moment was gone.

Victor hobbled to retrieve the ice pack. "Thanks, Brian. By the way, you were amazing in the championship game. That was fun to watch."

Brian scratched his head. "Uh, thanks."

Victor gave me a look, like *See, I can be nice to Brian.*

The rest of the night was strange. At first, Colby was rattled after whatever conversation happened between my mom and his mom, but eventually he calmed down a bit. He and Kevan seemed to have buried any lingering grudges, and they were teasing each other and laughing like old times. Colby and I didn't have any heart-to-hearts or anything, but he caught my eye a few times and smiled, and it was . . . OK, I guess. Once he looked from me to Victor and waggled his eyebrows, like he could sense that something happened between us. I blushed.

I didn't know what to do with the fact that Colby knew Victor liked me, and that he was OK with it. It was even weirder that he was the only one who knew. I felt guilty for keeping my friends in the dark.

I tried to pay more attention to Brian, now that the whole night had gone wonky, while paying just enough but not too much attention to Victor so no one suspected anything. Meanwhile, Ty was watching me like he was thinking *Are you OK right now, bruh?*

It was exhausting.

Before midnight, I rounded up blankets for Colby and Victor, and we spread out across the rec room. I offered Victor the couch, but he swore he was more comfortable on the floor. I ended up with Brian on my left and Victor on my right. We talked for a bit in the dark, but everyone fell quiet more quickly than usual. Soon Kevan was snoring softly across the room, and Brian's deep, even breathing told me he was asleep too.

On my other side, Victor tried to roll over and let out a pained grunt.

I slid closer to him. "You all right?" I whispered. "Sure you don't want anything?'

"I'm all right if I don't move too much," he answered. He settled on his back.

The room was quiet, but my heart was thumping loud enough that I could feel it in my ears. I slid my hand out in the dark until it found Victor's. His fingers curled around mine.

27. A MORTAL ENEMY LOVE STORY

BRIAN

Ezra's basement was still dark when I woke up to a gurgling in my guts. Just as I feared, Kevan's hot wings were haunting me. I slipped from my sleeping bag and rushed to the bathroom.

As I was tiptoeing back to my spot, trying not to wake anyone, I froze. Ezra was so close to Victor that his hair was grazing Victor's shoulder, and his hand was on Victor's arm.

Maybe Ezra just rolled over in his sleep. But it didn't look like an accident.

Ezra and Victor? *Together*? It seemed impossible . . . at first. If there was one thing my anxious brain was good at, it was storing up way too much information and overanalyzing every detail. It didn't take long to connect the dots.

Ezra + Victor: The Clues

1. *Ezra knew it was Victor playing piano a few weeks ago, before school.*
2. *Victor's a musician. There's nothing Ezra loves more than music.*
3. *Ezra's been working on the talent show for weeks. Victor's probably in the show too. Maybe they've been practicing together.*
4. *Ezra's mentioned more than once that Victor's changed.*
5. *Victor complimented me out of nowhere last night. Was he trying to impress Ezra?*
6. *That whole bathroom thing was weird. Like I'd interrupted . . .*
7. *What did I interrupt? Were they kissing?!*
8. *Maybe Ezra's keeping secrets. He's seemed more distant lately, like there are things he's not saying.*
9. *No, that's not fair. I've been more distant. I fell in a hole.*

As usual, thinking too much late at night led me to a bad place. But it was true: I'd missed a lot over the winter. I hadn't been the greatest friend.

It took a long time to fall back asleep.

In the morning, Ezra helped Victor gather his things. Victor was trying to play it cool, even though he was in obvious pain. Maybe it was rotten to find it annoying, but I couldn't help it. Yeah, it was brave what he did last night, but he didn't have to act all tough about it.

Ty, Kevan, and I waited downstairs while Ezra went upstairs with Colby and Victor when Colby's dad showed up. Without saying it, the rest of us decided we didn't want any part of that awkwardness.

Eventually, Ezra came back and told us breakfast was ready. Ezra's mom has made us scrambled eggs and Trinidadian bread called coconut bake. Ty inhaled two pieces. It was delicious, but I could only pick at mine. I wasn't that hungry.

Ezra noticed. He kept glancing at me. When his mom left the kitchen, he cleared his throat. "So . . . last night got kind of weird."

"Super weird," Kevan said. "It's good Colby thought to come here, though. And it was kind of nice to see him. Even if he brought Victor."

"Yeah." Ezra poked at his eggs.

I couldn't hold back the question burning in my gut. "What's the deal with you and Victor?"

Ezra went stiff. "What do you mean?"

"You know what I mean." It came out sharper than I expected, but his guilty expression confirmed the suspicions that had kept me awake.

"Wait. What's happening?" Kevan looked from me to Ezra. "Is this why you asked me about Victor? Please tell me you don't have a crush on him."

Ezra flinched.

"You do!" Kevan shook his head. "Ezra, really? You remember what he was like last year, right? I know he seems more chill now, and I respect what he did last night, but—"

"But it's hard to forget," I said.

The table went quiet.

Ezra let out a shaky breath. "I know. I never meant to keep it a secret. It all just . . . happened." He looked at me with pleading eyes. "I know what he did last year isn't OK. I never wanted to hurt you. But I didn't know how to tell you."

Flutters of anxiety rippled through my chest. "You spent all winter trying to get me to talk even when I didn't feel like it, but you don't tell me stuff because you don't think I can handle it. That's not fair."

Ezra was blinking a lot. Heat was building in my eyes too.

Before either of us could speak, Ty rose from the table. "We should go. Let you guys talk. Come on, Kev."

Kevan stood up slowly. My whole body started humming and I couldn't take it.

"I need to go too," I blurted out.

The devastation on Ezra's face made me feel like throwing up.

"I need time to think," I said. "We'll talk later."

"OK," he whispered.

The silence made my skin crawl as we packed our things. I could barely look at Ezra when he closed the door behind us. As we walked to the sidewalk, Ty stopped like he wanted to say something, but he just squeezed my shoulder before he turned toward his place.

The rest of the weekend was a wrestling match with the Green Goblin.

I didn't talk to Ezra. Every time I picked up my phone, I had too many confusing thoughts and worst-case scenarios scrolling through my mind, and I couldn't figure out what to say. So I avoided him as long as I could.

Monday morning homeroom was awkward.

"Hey," Ezra said.

"Hey," I said.

Ty frowned at us both. "Seriously? You two still haven't talked?"

"Um." I stared at the desk, but then "O Canada" started up on the PA and I was spared.

Ezra didn't push me to talk, even though I could tell my silence was making him miserable. He spent morning break in the music room, and he had a talent show meeting at lunch.

It was a relief that I got to skip last period and catch the bus to an appointment with Dr. Bender. She went skiing over March Break (I guess psychologists needed vacations too), so I hadn't seen her in two weeks. I filled her in on how I'd been feeling better and being more social lately. Mostly.

"That's great! I'm proud of you," Dr. Bender said. "I get the sense there's something else on your mind, though."

"Yeah." I swirled my tea bag in my mug. "It's one of those things that'll sound silly."

"Let's hear it."

"I think my best friend is in love with my mortal enemy."

"Well, that's not silly," Dr. Bender said. "It sounds like a great hook for a novel."

"Good point."

She smiled and waited for me to explain. I told her about the weekend, and how I'd pieced together all the things Ezra hadn't been telling me, and how hurt I'd felt ever since.

Dr. Bender sipped her tea. "Which part bothers you most? That he has feelings for someone you don't like, or that he didn't tell you about it?"

"I don't know," I admitted. "I mean, I know he didn't start crushing on Victor on purpose. And I get why he didn't want to tell me. He's always thinking about my feelings, and I want him to be happy, but . . . I guess I wish things were different."

"Different how?" Dr. Bender leaned forward. "You can tell me if I'm off base here, but I'm sensing maybe this isn't just about Ezra and Victor?"

"Maybe."

Dr. Bender waited. The thought I'd been pushing away sprung to the surface, and suddenly my eyes stung. The unexpected wave of emotion was a little embarrassing. But it wasn't like it was the first time I'd cried in Dr. Bender's office before, so I fought past the lump in my throat.

"I kissed him. Ezra, I mean. Back in November. And—I didn't really feel anything," I said. "He tried not to make it a big deal, but I know it hurt him. And then I accidentally set him up with Victor the day I passed out in school, and I was depressed all winter so naturally he wanted to hang out with Victor instead. I know I can't change any of those things, but it still feels like I made this happen. Like, maybe in an alternate universe, there's a Brian who felt something magic when he kissed Ezra, then he had a much better winter than I did, and they lived happily ever after."

"I see," Dr. Bender said. "So do you believe things would have been different if you had romantic feelings for Ezra?"

"I don't know. Maybe." I grabbed a tissue for my annoyingly leaky eyes. "But I just don't feel that way about anyone—not just Ezra. And it seems like one more way I'm different from my friends."

"That's understandable," Dr. Bender said. "You get bombarded with messages at your age about what you're supposed to feel and when, don't you?"

"Yeah."

"Well, I promise you that you aren't the only thirteen-year-old who isn't sure who they're attracted to—or if they're attracted to anyone at all. And some of your peers who feel one way now might come to a different understanding later in life. That's part of the human experience."

She offered me a kind smile. "And you, Brian Day, are a perfectly lovely human who has already dealt with an awful lot. This is another area where I'd encourage you to give yourself grace. Process your sexuality at your own pace."

"I guess that makes sense," I said. Hearing Dr. Bender say all that made me feel a little better.

"I'm glad," she said. "Now, do you want to talk more about the mortal enemy part?"

"Not really. I want to be over Victor. I thought I was. I mean, I'd barely thought about him for months until this weekend. But now I'm remembering all the awful things he did to me last year."

"That's natural too," Dr. Bender said.

"I know. We don't get over things all at once. You've told me that before."

"Glad to hear you're paying attention. I'm very wise, you know."

"Yeah. A little conceited, though." I smiled.

She laughed. "Fair enough. So, what do you want to do now?"

I exhaled. "I think I should talk to my best friend."

28. WORST-CASE SCENARIOS

EZRA

On Monday at lunch, Madi's smile kept growing as the crowd got bigger for our prep meeting for tomorrow night's talent show. The music room was so warm from all the bodies that Ms. Burtt had to open the window.

"Isn't this great?" Madi said to me. "I was worried that people wouldn't actually show up, but the show's going to be amazing!"

"Yeah," I said, but I didn't feel great. Today had been awful. Brian was barely talking to me. I might have blown it with him completely over Victor, and Victor wasn't here either. He hadn't texted since he left my house on Saturday. I kept telling myself he probably had a lot to deal with right now, but I couldn't help worrying that he had regrets about telling me that he liked me, and now he was avoiding me too.

Everything was a mess.

I was supposed to be helping Madi run this meeting, but I couldn't focus. Fortunately, she was on top of it. She went through the order with Ty, who'd volunteered to emcee the show, and she and Ms. Burtt gave instructions to everyone who was helping set up tomorrow. It all went fine, I guess, but as everyone cleared out, Madi turned to me.

"That's it. Victor's out. If he couldn't even show up today, we can't count on him tomorrow."

"Maybe we could give him a pass. I don't think he's in school today. He had, uh, a rough weekend."

"Right, 'cause he's a hero now." Madi rolled her eyes. "You believe all that?"

Word had gotten around about what Victor and Colby did on Friday. I guess a kid in the ninth grade had a sister who was there, though I suspected Colby did some talking too.

"I saw him," I said. "He and Colby came to my house. He was pretty beat up."

"Oh." Madi's expression softened.

"I'll text him. Make sure he's here tomorrow," I said with way more confidence than I felt.

"Fine." Madi sighed. "Look, it seems like you two are friends now, or . . . whatever." Her eyebrows raised on the *whatever*, and my face went hot.

"And I get it," she continued, putting her hand on my arm. "He seems great at first. But I know what he did to Alicia. I don't want that to happen to you."

"Uh, thanks," I said. "But I'm all right. Let's just focus on being awesome tomorrow."

"Deal. The whole show's going to be awesome, but we're going to be the most awesome." She gave me a high five and we headed to class.

I waited 'til the end of the day to text Victor. A flutter filled my chest as I typed.

Hey, missed you in school today. Everything OK?

It was embarrassing how relieved I felt when he replied right away.

Victor: Yeah, lots of family drama this weekend so Mom let me stay home. I'll be back tomorrow though

Me: Sounds intense. Want to talk about it?

Victor: Nah I'm OK. Thanks though

Me: Madi's worked up that you weren't at the talent show meeting but I told her you'll be there tomorrow for sure

Victor: I will. Looking forward to it

Thanks for having my back. You're the best

It was also embarrassing how many times I reread that last line. Then I got another text that made my stomach drop.

Brian: Can I come over? We should talk

Brian and I sat at opposite ends of the couch in my basement. Brian was hunched forward and fiddling with the necklace Richie had given him for a birthday present last year, so I knew he was nervous. I didn't want to rush him, but I couldn't take the silence anymore.

"It's OK if you're mad," I said. "I get it. I shouldn't have—"

"Ezra," he cut me off. He took a deep breath. "Do you want to hear my worst-case scenario?"

"Uh . . . sure?"

Brian closed his eyes. "Victor turns you to the dark side, you start hating me, and you both pick on me. Like last year, but ten times worse."

My jaw dropped. "Brian, I'd never. You know that."

"I do. Honestly." He opened his eyes. "But that's something Dr. Bender helped me with. If I lean all the way into my worst-case scenarios until they get ridiculous, then they're less scary."

"Oh." I adjusted my glasses. "Well, want to hear my worst-case scenario then?"

"Of course."

I swallowed. "Victor turns out to be a disaster, but you and Kevan and Ty and Madi are so mad at me that you never forgive me, and I end up with no friends at all."

"That's not going to happen either. I promise." Brian ran a hand through his hair. "Look, I get why you didn't tell me. And Victor and I will probably never be, like, BFFs or anything, but I'll try not to be weird about it if you like him."

I was so relieved Brian wasn't mad that I couldn't stop myself from grinning. "Victor can't be your BFF. I've claimed that role for life."

"For *life*? Bold of you."

"You know the last *F* stands for *Forever*, right? It's literally there in the title."

Brian smiled too. Then he fiddled with his necklace again. "So . . . I saw Dr. Bender today, and one thing she helped me figure out was that I wasn't just worked up about you and Victor. I was still feeling bad about how I let you down when we kissed."

My face went hot. "That's not your fault."

"I know. But we should have talked about it more, I think." He looked me in the eye. "It hurt, right?"

I swallowed. "Yeah. But I didn't want to make a big deal of it, because . . ."

"I know." Brian slid closer to me. "But you don't have to protect my feelings, OK? You can tell me stuff too."

"Right." Warmth filled my chest. "I want to show you something."

I led him to my room and brought my laptop to my bed. I played the track I'd recorded with Victor at his apartment, the night I first figured out I was crushing on him.

"You made that together?" Brian said when it was done. "It's amazing."

"Recording together is super fun," I said. "It's weird, though. We don't talk much at school, but he's different when it's just the two of us. Friday was the first time he told me how he really feels."

Brian grinned. "You mean in the bathroom? Did you guys kiss?"

I cough. "No . . . but we were going to. Maybe."

"Oh! Sorry I ruined the moment."

"That's OK," I said. "It was a weird moment. And a weird night."

"No kidding."

"Now that I think about it, I'm kind of glad our first kiss wasn't in the same place where I poop."

Brian snorted, and we both started laughing. When we caught our breath, he looked over at my guitar in the corner.

"So . . . do I get a sneak preview of your song for the talent show?"

I sighed. "You really want to hear it?"

"Ezra, are you kidding?"

"OK. But you have to tell me if it sucks."

"It's not going to suck." He shoved me toward my guitar. "Just play."

So I did.

I went to bed Monday night feeling a million times better after talking to Victor and patching things up with Brian, but on Tuesday it hit me hard that I was going to be performing in front of a whole lot of people tonight. My body buzzed and I couldn't keep my hands still. My fingers ran through riffs and chord patterns all day.

When school finally ended, I stayed to help set up to keep busy. Ms. Burtt directed traffic, but Madi was in charge, marching around the cafeteria with a clipboard. Some silver streamers, strands of white Christmas lights, and fake candles from the dollar store did a surprisingly good job of giving the place some atmosphere. With the fluorescent lights off and the room bathed in a soft glow, I could almost forget this was the same room where Colby once burped the first lines of "O Canada."

"You're really good at this," I told Madi. "You could be an event planner."

"Thank you!" She smiled, then her eyes narrowed as Caleb knocked over a stack of chairs with a crash. She gathered her breath to yell, but I put a hand on her shoulder.

"Save your voice. We're supposed to be having fun, remember?"

"Right." She exhaled and went to deal with the mess.

I headed back to the band room to tune my guitar. I was fiddling with my high E string when a voice said, "Sounds good to me."

I looked up. Victor crossed the room stiffly, like he was still sore.

"How are you?" I asked.

He shrugged. "Feeling better, looking worse."

"No kidding," I said. His eye was purplish yellow, and the lid was swollen. "How're your ribs?"

He half smiled. "You want another peek under my shirt?"

"Shut up." My cheeks went warm, but I couldn't help laughing. Victor's grin got bigger.

"Anyway, good luck," he said. "Not that you need it. You'll be great."

"You too. Uh, you will too. You know what I mean." My face grew even hotter.

Victor chuckled. Neither of us moved. The air felt . . . tingly.

A group of kids walked past the band room, and Victor turned. When he looked back at me, the grin was gone. He coughed. "Well, see you out there." He left me to gather my gear.

My head felt light as I made my way back to the cafeteria. The room was filling up. Kevan and Brian waved from the table where they were selling Kev's baked goods. Ty strutted in, dressed in a crisp black suit with a lime-green tie and retro Jordans to match. Of course he was going to run the show in style.

A hand clapped on my shoulder, and I turned to see Gabe and Brittany. "Ready to rock out?" Gabe asked.

I blinked. "I didn't know you guys were coming."

"We wouldn't miss it!" Brittany said. "We have to catch you now, before you're famous and tickets are, like, fifty bucks."

I laughed. "I'll always save you free passes."

"You'd better." Brittany lightly punched my arm, and she and Gabe went to sit with Mrs. Clelland. I headed to the front of the room and found Madi scanning the crowd. My parents came in, and I gave them a quick wave.

Madi drew in a tight breath. "There're a lot of people here. Are you nervous?"

"Yeah, a little." My eyes drifted to Victor, sitting at a table with Colby and their buddies. I didn't tell Madi that my nerves had changed direction. I was less worried about performing now that I was thinking about how I'd really like to kiss Victor.

"Good evening, humans of Halifax," Ty said in a silky-smooth voice, and the show began. Ms. Burtt directed a small ensemble from the ninth-grade band through a few pieces to open, then we got a juggler, and a dance routine to "Single Ladies." Caleb and Nneka did a drum-and-bass jam that had the whole room clapping along. I couldn't stop grinning as I watched Caleb with his arms flying and his tongue poking out of his mouth. He and Nneka were good. Like, *maybe we should start a band together* good.

In between acts, Ty told jokes and roasted teachers. He scanned the crowd and pointed out our science teacher. "Folks, you know this is a special night, because

Mr. Harding is rocking his pink argyle sweater vest. He usually wears gray on Tuesdays, maybe maroon if he's feeling extra fly, but pink argyle? Whew!" Ty fanned himself. "That bad boy only comes out on Worm Dissection Day. You're wild tonight, Mr. H. Don't sell that man any more fudge, Kevan. He's cut off."

Everyone was cracking up, even Mr. Harding. I caught Mrs. Clelland wiping tears of laughter. Ty's jokes also helped keep everyone loose, which was great, because I didn't have time to get really nervous again before I was up with Madi. Once we took the stage, she drew a breath and I started the intro of "Blackbird." We'd practiced together enough now that we were totally in sync, and playing for a crowd was fun. Madi sounded great, and I didn't screw up, and everyone cheered when we were done. Madi beamed and gave me a side-hug. I heard a couple whistles, which was annoying but it could have been worse, I guess. Madi blushed as we walked off the stage together.

Then it was Victor's turn.

After Ty introduced him, he walked straight to the piano and began to play. I thought he'd do one of his own pieces, but he chose "Moonlight Sonata" instead. For a guy who hardly ever showed what he was feeling, he sure could make a piano sound tragic and haunting. The room hushed as he played. When he finished on a low, soft minor chord, I got goose-bumps and the room was silent until he lifted his hands from the keys and people applauded. I couldn't see many people's expressions in the dimmed

room, but I glanced at Madi and she was blinking in surprise. Even Ty fumbled out a "Well, *dang*," before he dove
back into his script.

I watched Victor settle back at his table. I wonder if
Colby said anything besides "Good job, bro."

I was still thinking about his performance when Ty
said, "And now it's time for the man, the myth, the legend,
Ezra Komizarek!"

Startled, I nearly tripped over my feet as I hopped up.
Not a great start. My heart thumped as I plugged my guitar into my amp and stepped to the mic. I was way more
chill backing up Madi, but now I felt exposed. The spotlight made my forehead sweat. For a second I was flat-out
terrified.

"You got this!" Brian's voice rang out.

A few people chuckled. They probably didn't even know
what it meant for Brian of all people to yell out in a crowded
room like that. I couldn't even see him in the dark, but I
instantly felt lighter. I drew in a breath.

"This is, um, a song I wrote," I said. Then I closed my
eyes and started to play.

29. ELECTRIC

BRIAN

Ezra was electric.

The instant he started playing, he went into Avatar mode and harnessed all his powers at once. His voice was full of soul as he sang about holding on when the winter was long.

I was glad I got a preview last night, otherwise I'd have been a mess. I still felt a lump in my throat. It wasn't a song about me, exactly, but it was about us, about everything, and it was incredible. Tonight, it was even more amazing watching him in the spotlight, playing to a full crowd. He started quiet and built until he stomped on his distortion pedal and his guitar got all loud and crunchy, and Brittany let out a whoop from somewhere near the front. Ezra beamed.

He looked so *alive*.

Kevan nudged me with his elbow. He was recording with his phone, and he gave me a wide-eyed grin, like *Holy smokes, right?* I looked around. Ty was nodding at the edge of the stage with a massive grin on his face. Brittany had her arms in the air. People all over the room were into it. A lot of talented kids had played tonight—I was still trying to wrap my head around Victor's performance—but Ezra was special. He had the Sizzle Sauce.

When he finished, letting a last thundering chord ring out, we all went wild.

30. ALL THE WRONG THINGS

EZRA

I felt like I was dreaming as the cheers washed over me. The loudest was probably my mom, though I couldn't quite make her out near the back. I practically floated off the stage, and I didn't get far before Brittany wrapped me in a huge hug. I was grinning so wide, I could feel it in my cheeks. The applause felt amazing, but more than that, I was thrilled because I *did it*. And once I'd started, it wasn't scary. I felt like I belonged up there. I already wanted to do it again.

The school band closed with a performance of the *Jurassic Park* theme, and then Ms. Burtt took the mic to thank Ty for hosting and Madi and me for organizing the show. After more applause, the lights came up and the room filled with the noise of conversations and scraping chairs. My friends rushed over, and Brian gave me a big hug.

"Ezra, that was incredible!" he said. "I mean, I knew it would be, but *wow*."

"You weren't just great, you were a whole vibe," Brittany said. "I'm so proud of you, dude."

"I recorded it all," Kevan added. "We *have* to get you a YouTube channel."

"Slow down, Kev," I laughed. I was still giddy from the thrill of playing.

Caleb ran up to us. "Ezra! You're like the wickedest guitarist! And you have an amazing voice! We should start a band. You and me and Nneka and Victor and Madi. We would be *awesome*."

"I was thinking the same thing," I told him.

"Really?" Caleb got so excited, he threw his arms in the air, and his drumsticks went flying. "Whoops! Anyway, that's cool! Talk to you tomorrow!" He fled as quickly as he arrived, chasing after his sticks.

Ty watched him and shook his head. "Your rock-star hotness is a powerful thing, my friend. That boy has the biggest crush on you."

I blinked. "Caleb?"

"Definitely," Gabe chimed in. "Brittany's right about your vibe. I bet a bunch of kids fell in love with you tonight."

It was a flattering thought, but right now I was only interested in one person who had a crush on me. Victor was still across the room, talking with his friends. I was trying to suck up the courage to go over when Ms. Burtt beckoned him to the front of the room. I took the chance to join them.

"Can you wheel the piano back to the music room?" Ms. Burtt was asking Victor. "Maybe one of your friends can help—"

"I'll do it," I volunteered. Victor gave me a half smile.

We each grabbed an end and steered the piano toward the exit. The crowd parted for us, and then we were in the hallway, alone. Victor guided the front of the piano, backpedaling and looking over his shoulder as he went. A lock of hair fell across his forehead every time he turned.

He caught me looking and half grinned again. "What?"

My cheeks went hot. "Did you ever think about learning the harmonica? It's much more portable."

Victor laughed. "How do you know I'm not a harmonica genius?"

"I guess I don't. Maybe it's part of your mysterious past."

I was joking, mostly, but Victor only went "Heh" and looked back over his shoulder. When we reached the music room, we parked the piano, and he leaned against his side.

"Is that how you think of me? That I'm mysterious?"

I shrugged. "You don't tell me much."

He was quiet for a moment. "You were amazing tonight," he said eventually.

"You were too," I said.

"Thanks, but you were *really* great. And brave." He exhaled. "I thought about playing something I wrote, but I chickened out. You did it, though. And it was incredible. Watching you perform tonight . . ."

Victor drifted closer with each word, until we were both standing in front of the piano. I took his hand. He squeezed mine back. My heart was thumping hard against my ribs.

Victor pushed his hair from his face. He swallowed. "Ezra, I, um . . ."

Just kiss me. Or maybe I should kiss you.

Then we heard laughter echoing down the hall, and Victor let go of my hand like it had burned him. He took a half step away as band kids poured in, carrying instruments and stands.

It stung.

As the room filled with people and voices, Madi and Miranda rushed to me and started talking. By the time I looked up, Victor was following Colby out the door. He glanced back and gave me the tiniest nod before he was gone.

Everything was hazy after that. A bunch more people congratulated me when I headed back to the cafeteria to pack up my guitar and amp. On the drive home, Mom and Dad told me how proud they were and how great I'd sounded. I smiled through it all, but my mind was stuck on how Victor dropped my hand in an instant.

Once I was in my room, I opened our chat and stared at my phone, hoping he might say something. Apologize even. But he didn't.

On Wednesday morning, I wasn't sure if I wanted to find Victor or avoid him. I had no idea which would make the flutter in my belly go away. But I didn't run into him before homeroom, and the flutter was still there when I plopped into my seat.

Brian leaned toward me. "Are you OK?" he asked softly.

I wanted to explain, but not here, not when I still needed to make it through school. "I don't know," I whispered back. "I'll tell you later."

By second period, I'd decided I didn't want to keep riding this roller coaster where Victor and I went from good to awkward and back again. I needed to know if he was for real. At morning break, I went looking for him. It didn't take long. As I entered the stairwell, a group of guys rushed past, with Victor at the back of the pack.

"Wait up," he wheezed. "My ribs still hurt."

"Victor," I called.

He slowed. When his eyes met mine, my stomach plunged.

Victor looked afraid.

Like he was worried I'd blurt out *Hey, why didn't you kiss me last night?* in front of his cool friends.

Maybe there was some other reason. Whatever. It was definitely fear in his eyes, and it made me feel so small.

He recovered quickly. "Hey," he said casually. "Can we catch up later? After school?"

"You coming?" one of the guys yelled at the bottom of the stairs. Colby met my eyes for a split second and looked away. Victor turned toward them, and I knew where he wanted to be.

"Go ahead," I mumbled.

"OK. Talk later." He did the freaking *nod* again and hurried down the stairs.

I headed to the bathroom and stayed there until break was over.

I managed to hold it together through the next two periods. But at lunch, Victor's crew was in the foyer. There was no way to reach the cafeteria without passing them, and it was the last thing I wanted to do. I was itchy all over, sweat broke out on my forehead, and everything sounded ten times louder than usual.

I grabbed Brian's arm. "Can we do lunch at your house? Like right now?"

Brian didn't hesitate. "Let's go."

I headed for the side doors, avoiding the foyer and front doors altogether. Brian didn't ask why, or why we weren't stopping for our coats. He waited until we were a block from school before he asked, "What's wrong? You look how I feel when I'm having a panic attack."

I scratched my neck. The itch still lingered, but I felt less like I might spontaneously combust now that we were outside.

"I felt gross all of a sudden," I admitted. "I had to get out of there."

Brian was quiet for half a block. "Victor?"

"Yeah."

He waited. Brian was the last person who'd rush someone into spilling their guts.

After a few more steps, I told him how quickly Victor had changed last night, and how he'd brushed me off this morning. "I feel like such a dope. Madi warned me. I should have known better."

He sighed. "I'm so sorry, Ezra."

He meant it too. Even though he had every reason to say, *Duh, I knew this would happen,* he only looked sad. Because he cared about me that much.

Hanging out at his house made me feel a little better. We had PE last period, and running around the gym helped me blow off steam too. At the end of the day, Brian and I made it without running into Victor again, but we were three blocks from school when I heard him calling behind us.

"Ezra! Wait!"

The itch on my neck returned. Brian noticed.

"You could pretend you didn't hear him," he murmured.

But I couldn't. Not really. With a sigh, I looked back. Victor and Colby were rushing toward us. When they caught up, no one spoke for a moment that probably lasted three seconds but contained enough awkwardness to fill a whole week.

"I thought we were going to talk after school," Victor said.

That was where he was starting? Not even *Good to see you* or *Sorry I acted like I barely know you*?

I shrugged. "You weren't specific, so I made plans with Brian."

"Oh." Victor glanced around like he was making sure no one was listening, and I hated it. "Maybe tonight?"

"Nah. I'm good." I started walking.

"Ezra?" Victor's voice went . . . not angry, exactly, but there was an edge to it that I didn't like.

I stopped and folded my arms. "You acted like you didn't want to be seen with me last night, and today. And I don't want to keep doing that. So just give me some space, please."

He frowned. "Ezra, it's not like that."

"What's it like, then? Please explain."

Victor's mouth twitched like his words were stuck. His eyes cut to Brian.

"You can talk in front of Brian," I said. "He's my best friend. And he knows about us."

Victor's cheeks went red.

"Brian would never out you," I continued. "And neither would I, if that's what you're worried about. I understand if you're not ready, and I'd never pressure you about that. But I'm not going to pretend we're strangers, either. It doesn't feel good."

Victor looked at his shoes. "I don't want that either. It's just . . . you don't understand."

"How am I supposed to understand? You bury everything, and never talk about what's really going on with you, and I can't keep doing that either. You need to figure some stuff out. Then maybe we can talk."

I started down the sidewalk with Brian. He didn't stop us. For five seconds I hoped he'd run after me, say he was sorry, and pour out a heartfelt confession like the love interest coming to his senses in a rom-com. But he didn't.

I glanced back. His shoulders were slumped, and he and Colby were just standing there. They were letting us get ahead, I guess, since Colby lived one street away from me and it was way too awkward to walk together now.

"Do you know what your problem is?" I called. "This goes for you too, Colby. You both act like you're too cool to care about anything, but you care just as much as the rest of us. You just care about all the wrong things."

Colby stretched his arms like he was saying *What did I do?* Victor just blinked.

I turned and stormed away.

31. ADVANCED DOUBLES MOPING

BRIAN

Ezra stomped home like he was trying to fight the sidewalk. I didn't know what to say, but it felt like I should give him space. I stayed quiet until we reached his house, and he plopped onto a stool in the kitchen.

I sat beside him. "That was impressive. You handled that well."

"Yeah? Then why do I feel like garbage?" He wiped at his eyes.

I wanted so badly to make him feel better. Whenever I was down, Ezra always tried to pick me up. He and Gabe and Brittany had nudged me out of so many holes, and even when I fell in a colossal, planet-eating hole, they were there all the way. I wasn't always great at accepting their help, but I knew I could count on them.

Then it hit me. I knew what to do. I put a hand on his shoulder. "This is where I should say something encouraging. But honestly, you deserve to mope all afternoon."

He sniffle-laughed. "You think?"

"Definitely. Lucky for you, I'm a junior regional champion moper. Wallowing in misery is one of my greatest talents. I'm usually a solo moper, but today we could practice advanced doubles moping."

"How does that work?"

"Hmm." I paced the kitchen like a coach hashing out game strategy. "We need comfort food, starting with drinks. Hot chocolate?"

"Mom says ginger tea fixes everything," Ezra said. "But I could do hot chocolate."

"Good. And we need to pair that with more sugar." I rooted through the pantry and found a box of Jos Louis cakes. "Are we allowed to eat these?" Before he could answer, I held up a hand. "Trick question. When you're dealing with heartache, you can eat whatever you want."

I filled the kettle to boil water. "I'll make drinks. You go change. You can't mope in jeans."

"What do you recommend?"

"In a hardcore mope, I strip to my underwear and cocoon in a blanket. But if you don't want to go that bleak, just pick your most comfortable clothes." I gestured to the sweatpants and hoodie I'd worn to school. "As you can see, I'm always prepared."

Ezra headed to his room. I'd just put the finishing touches on two perfect mugs of hot chocolate when he returned in pajama pants and a basketball warm-up shirt.

"Perfect," I said. "Now, we could watch one of your favorite TV episodes to unwind while we snack, or we could jump right to the musical portion of our program."

Ezra's eyes lit up. "How about one episode of *Avatar* while I make a playlist?"

I nodded. "You're definitely ready for advanced doubles moping."

By the time we finished the beach episode of *Avatar*, Ezra had assembled a masterful mix of melancholy on his phone. He connected it to the speakers in his room and we chilled for a while without talking, just letting the music wash over us. Ezra closed his eyes and mumble-sang along. I joined him in my best falsetto, and he laughed.

Ezra lay back on his bed. "Maybe I should be a monk. Maybe that's easier than crushing on anyone."

"I don't think that would help. I think you'd just be a monk who has crushes." I stretched beside him. "Maybe you need to find someone halfway between Victor and me. We're both disasters in different ways. Maybe there's someone who has our good qualities with none of the messy side effects. Or you could combine our DNA in a lab."

"That sounds like a setup for a zombie movie. Try to engineer the perfect guy, then he eats your brain."

"You should write a song about it. Like a shouty punk song."

Ezra sat up. He smiled.

Five minutes later, he was playing noisy power chords while we both yelled, "*I fell in love with a zombie / And he tried to eat my braaaain!*" That was the only lyric we had, but sometimes songs didn't need to be complicated.

Besides, writing a song was a top-tier achievement in advanced doubles moping. Ezra and I were pros.

32. VISITED BY GHOSTS

EZRA

By the time we finished rocking out about zombies, I was sweaty and laughing. "You're an expert moping coach," I told Brian. "This helped a lot."

"I'm glad." Brian threw an arm around me. "We're good, right?"

We're good could mean a lot of things. Maybe he was talking about our zombie song, but I thought back to the awkwardness after our kiss, the hard months of winter, and all the things we didn't know how to say. None of that had been in the way today. Telling Brian everything had been easy. And it made me realize that my feelings had changed. Maybe I'd always have a little bit of a crush on Brian, but today, he was my best friend who had my back when I felt lousy, and it was exactly what I needed. It was all I needed.

I leaned against his shoulder. "Yeah. We're good."

After Brian left, I checked my phone. I had messages from Ty and Kevan checking in on me, which was sweet. Madi wrote to thank me again for helping with the talent show, and Caleb texted So when are we starting a band?!!!!!!! I had to laugh at the seven exclamation points.

There was also a message from Victor.

You were right about today, and last night.

I'm sorry. I want to make it right.

I thought about responding for five seconds, then I put my phone away. If he was serious about making it right, he'd know a text wasn't enough.

He didn't try to find me in school on Thursday. I didn't see him until the end of the day, when I spotted him in Mrs. Clelland's classroom. They were alone, having what looked like a serious conversation. I was curious, but it wasn't my business so I stayed out of it.

The next morning in homeroom, I was only half paying attention to the announcements over the intercom when I caught Ms. Floriman say, "And finally, we have a special announcement from one of our students, Victor MacLennan."

My neck prickled.

"Hey," Victor's voice boomed out of the speaker, and a few kids in homeroom giggled. Someone must have told him to back off the mic, because he resumed more softly. "I asked Ms. Floriman if I could have a minute, because I need to apologize."

Instantly the giggles turn to whispers. Brian, Ty, and I looked at each other.

"I made a big mistake this week," Victor said. "And I hurt someone I really like. I won't embarrass them, but they know who they are."

The whispers around us got louder. My face burned and I dropped my eyes to my desk.

"I also want them to know that they're right," Victor said. "I've been caring about the wrong things. But I really do care about you. And I hope you'll give me another chance. If it's not right away, I understand."

"Aw!" a girl named Sara said a row away from me. "That's so romantic! I wonder who he's talking about?"

Victor kept going. "But I need to say sorry to a lot of people. And it's not enough to say one big *sorry* over the intercom. So, if I was mean to you over the last year and a half, I want to apologize, in person. Come see me in Mrs. Clelland's room at lunch today."

Suddenly everyone was talking. Ms. Virth held up her hands for quiet, but even she had a shocked expression on her face.

"If you think this sounds like a prank, I don't blame you," Victor said. "But I asked permission from Ms. Floriman, and Mrs. Clelland will be there, so please come if I owe you an apology. Uh, that's it. Thanks for listening."

Everyone was still buzzing after the bell rang.

Ty grinned as we made our way to first-period French. "Wow. Victor has it *bad* for you, Ezra. He's out here trying to make amends like Ebenezer Scrooge. Maybe he was visited by ghosts last night."

Brian scowled. "I don't trust him."

"So you're not going at lunch?" Ty asked.

Brian shrugged. "What do you think, Ezra?"

"I don't know what to think." That was the truth. I couldn't decide if I was glad or annoyed that he'd chosen to apologize like this. I guess it was one way to show he wasn't being secretive anymore. Still, I wasn't sure what to make of it all.

Kevan caught up with us at the break, and of course he was brimming with news.

"I think Victor's serious," he said in a low voice, as if everyone in the hall wasn't talking about the exact same thing. "Dude's looked terrified all morning. But he asked if I was coming. He said he owes me an apology for everything last year."

"Maybe you should go," Ty said. "Putting himself out there like that takes guts. You too, Ezra. Doesn't mean you have to give him another chance. Just see how it goes."

"Of course I'm going," Kevan said. "I need to know how this plays out. What about you, Brian?"

Brian looked down. "I don't know. Maybe."

I straightened my glasses. "I did tell Victor that if he's trying to do better, he needs to own up to everything he did last year. So I guess I should go and see what happens. But if it doesn't feel right, Brian, you don't have to go. You don't owe him anything."

The bell rang before Brian could answer. But the look on his face told me he still wasn't sure.

33. HOW TO SHED A DRAGON SKIN

BRIAN

I didn't want to think about Victor. But I couldn't think about anything else.

Seven minutes before lunch, I told Mrs. Woolaver I had to use the bathroom. If anyone else asked, she'd probably make them wait until lunch, but she'd gone easier on me since I passed out in the hall during her quiz, and I didn't mind milking that guilt.

I headed to Mrs. Clelland's room, hoping to catch her before Victor arrived. But he was already there, helping Mrs. Clelland move desks and set up chairs in a circle. Mrs. Clelland must have had a prep period, because there was no one else in the room.

I hesitated by the door. My gut screamed at me to leave and avoid the whole thing. But I took a breath and stepped inside.

"Hi Brian," Mrs. Clelland said softly.

Victor went pale when he saw me, which was a first. "Uh, hey. I wasn't sure if you'd come. But I'm glad you did."

Now that we were face-to-face, the wheel of emotion spinning in my brain landed on *anger*.

"I didn't come for your game," I said. "Whatever this is, I know you're only doing it to try to impress Ezra. Quit playing and leave him alone."

Victor's face fell, and so did Mrs. Clelland's.

"Brian," she said, with caution this time.

Suddenly I was angry with her too for going along with this, when she knew how awful Victor was to me last year. Maybe I was angry at myself too, for caring so much. I wanted to be over it, but a ton of memories and feelings bubbled up, and everything came pouring out.

"He's just acting to get what he wants," I told Mrs. Clelland. "He's always done this. He smiles and says the right things when teachers are watching, but he's poison." I turned to Victor, my voice rising. "If you actually cared about Ezra, you'd stay away and stop messing with him. He might be the nicest person in this whole school. You don't deserve him, and you know it!"

Mrs. Clelland gasped. "Brian!"

I couldn't look at her. I was already ashamed that I was yelling. I waited for Victor to lose his temper or say something awful to me. But he didn't. He sighed.

"You're right. Ezra is incredible, and I don't deserve him. But I . . ." His eyes drifted past my shoulder, and his face went even paler. Without turning, I knew Ezra had entered the room.

Victor's voice dropped to a whisper. "I have to try. I don't know what else to do."

Ezra stood beside me. The bell hadn't rung yet, so he must have played his *get out of jail free* card with Mrs. Woolaver too. He probably told her he was checking on me.

He put a hand on my shoulder. "You OK?"

I nodded. I couldn't stop looking at Victor, and the way he was looking at Ezra.

One thing I couldn't stand about Victor last year was how he always wore this aggravating smirk, like everything was one big joke. It was pretty freaking sweet when Ezra called him out for pretending he was too cool to care. But that cover was gone now. He was staring at Ezra with a love-sick *I'd give up a kidney for you* glaze in his eyes.

Mrs. Clelland took a step toward us. "Brian, Victor came to me wanting to make up for what he did to you, and to others. I thought a restorative approach might work, where he talks with the people he's hurt and takes responsibility for his actions. But if that doesn't feel helpful for you, that's completely OK. You don't have to participate."

"I don't blame you if you don't believe me," Victor said. "You can just stay and watch if you want. But I really am sorry, Brian."

I didn't want to let him off the hook, like he could say a magic word and fix everything. "You weren't sorry last year.

You *liked* making me miserable. Some nights I couldn't sleep because I felt so anxious about dealing with you the next day."

Ezra squeezed my shoulder.

Victor winced. "You're right. For a long time, I wasn't sorry. I told myself it wasn't a big deal. But obviously it was, because you were mad enough to break my nose."

"And I apologized. At Ty's party."

"That's what got me. Everyone was so glad you stood up to me, and the way you did it . . ." Victor swallowed. "Everyone loves when the good guy beats the bad guy, and it was obvious I was the bad guy. I *was* poison."

No kidding, I almost snapped back. Before I could decide whether I wanted to go through with this, the bell rang. Instantly there was a crowd at the door, like kids had sprinted here to grab a seat. They kept coming, until half the eighth grade and a handful of ninth graders were squished into Mrs. Clelland's room. Victor was trying to keep cool, but he looked ready to throw up. I couldn't lie, I enjoyed that part.

Colby crossed the room and stood with Victor. Ty and Kevan made their way to Ezra and me. When the room was full, Mrs. Clelland signaled for quiet.

"Before we start, how many people have something they want to address with Victor?"

Alicia's hand shot up. She fixed Victor with a laser stare. Four other hands followed, including Kevan's. I kept mine at my side. I still didn't know about this.

Mrs. Clelland glanced at me. "How many people might have something, but they're feeling unsure about how this is all going to work?"

Two more people slowly raised their hands. Ezra looked at me and lifted his hand. I swallowed and raised mine too.

Mrs. Clelland surveyed the rest of the group. "And how many just came to watch?"

There was a lot of shuffling and murmuring, and gradually everyone else raised their hands.

"Right. I appreciate your interest, but my classroom can't hold such a crowd, and this isn't meant to be a spectator sport. So please go enjoy your lunch."

More shuffling and grumbling, but Mrs. Clelland could put on a serious teacher stare when she needed to. The crowd thinned. Ty started to leave too.

"Wait." Everyone looked at me, and my faced burned. I still didn't love speaking in crowds. But I focused Mrs. Clelland. "I'd like Ty to stay. For moral support."

Mrs. Clelland looked at Victor. He shrugged.

"That's fair. Colby's here for me. And I did crash your party last year, Ty."

Ty scoffed. "Please. I'm not mad over that. No one can ruin a Ty Marsman party."

Everyone giggled, lightening the mood a little.

"I want Madi to stay too. For the same reason." Alicia glared at Victor again.

He gulped. "OK."

Mrs. Clelland ushered us into the circle. There were fourteen of us, including Mrs. Clelland, Victor, Colby, Ty, and Madi. That meant nine of us were there because Victor had messed with us somehow. Besides Ezra and Alicia, most of the others had been in my homeroom last year. I was Victor's favorite target, but I wasn't his only target.

Mrs. Clelland set her hands on her knees. "Welcome, everyone. We've never tried anything quite like this before, but I think it could be a good way to resolve conflicts. Thank you for being brave enough to take part. And thank you, Victor, for being willing to take ownership of your behavior."

She paused. The circle was dead silent.

"To do this well, we're going to have a few ground rules," she said. "Everyone will have a chance to share. I understand it may be hard for some of you, and you can say as much or as little as you want, while being mindful of our time. I'm going to ask that you speak about your experiences, without making value judgments on Victor as a person. And we are still in school, so please be respectful in your language."

A few people giggled. We understood: We couldn't just curse Victor out for an hour.

"One other important rule," Mrs. Clelland continued. "Everyone owns their story, and their story only. Victor will have a chance to respond and apologize, but we're not going to tell other people's stories, and we're not going to share anything we hear today outside of this room. Understood?"

Everyone nodded.

She turned to Victor. "Do you want to say anything before we start?"

Victor kept his eyes on the floor. "Thanks for coming. I, uh . . . I should have done this a while ago. But I was scared, I guess. I know I was a bully, and—well, I don't have any excuses. And I know that just saying it doesn't count for much, so I'm also going to start tutoring in math and science on Tuesdays at lunch. To try to do something good, I guess." He pushed a strand of hair from his face. "Anyway, we can go ahead now."

Kevan raised his hand. "Are we supposed to talk about the stuff you did, then you apologize? Is that how this works?"

Victor nodded. "Basically, yeah. Do you want to go first?"

"I guess." Kevan folded his arms over his chest. "You called me 'Captain Curry' when I brought samosas for lunch, and you made fun of how my food smelled. You know that's kinda racist, right? Maybe you thought it was just a joke—that's what Colby said when he covered for you." Kevan glared at Colby, who slumped in his seat. "But it wasn't funny. It sucked."

Victor's eyes dropped. "I know. I'm sorry."

"The worst part is, I let it bother me so much I stopped bringing good lunches to school." Kevan hunched forward. "I ate boring sandwiches like some basic white kid, just so you wouldn't make fun of me. No offense to all you white kids."

Ezra snickered, and Ty had a sudden coughing fit into his sleeve.

"I'm really sorry, Kevan," Victor said. "I bet your samosas were way better than my basic white-guy sandwiches."

"Yeah, they were," Kevan said. "And I shouldn't have let you ruin my lunch. I know better now."

"Maybe you'll let me try one sometime?" Victor said.

"You have to earn samosa privileges, dude." Kevan sat up straighter. "But we'll see."

Victor looked around. "Would someone else like to go?"

Matt Garrison raised his hand. "You called me Fat Matt." His voice shook. "I stopped eating my favorite foods too. Sometimes I didn't bring lunch at all. And I hated changing for gym. I hid in a stall, because you . . ."

Matt had to stop and swallow hard.

Victor turned bone white. "I'm sorry, Matt. I was mean and wrong."

The thing was, I felt a churning in my gut too. I glanced at the other kids who'd been in our gym class, and I was pretty sure we were all thinking the same thing: *We were there too.* We knew Matt disappeared into a stall. Colby snickered about it with Victor, but the rest of us pretended we didn't notice.

I'd been afraid of Victor. I'd been afraid to speak up. So I hadn't told a teacher or done anything to help Matt, just like he hadn't helped me.

Matt was staring at his shoes. Victor cleared his throat.

"You know, you're a killer artist. I remember those self-portraits we did in class last year, and yours was amazing."

Matt looked up. "Thanks," he said slowly.

"I remember that too," I added. "You're really talented, Matt."

Everyone looked at me. My face caught fire. "Sorry. I know we're not supposed to comment."

Mrs. Clelland paused for a moment. "Maybe a quick round of compliments would be all right, to validate people after they share."

"Your art is great, Matt," Miranda Wong weighed in. "And you're a good person, too. I hope you know you don't have to change for anyone else. *Especially* not for tiny people with their own problems." She glared at Victor.

"Thanks," Matt said.

A few other people said nice things too, and by the end, Matt was smiling.

Kevan raised his hand. "Wait, hello? We didn't do that for me."

Ty placed a hand over his heart. "I solemnly swear that Kevan's the best chef in this entire school."

"It's true," Colby said. "Especially your cookies. They're *the best*."

Kevan nodded. "Thank you. I feel validated now. You may continue."

Mrs. Clelland shook her head, biting back a smile. She caught my eye and mouthed *Thank you* before looking around the circle. "Would someone else like to go?"

Miranda stood up. "I'll go. As in, I'm leaving. I was curious how this would work, but I'm over Victor's whole deal, and honestly, I don't want to help him feel better about himself."

She started for the door.

"Miranda?" Mrs. Clelland half rose from her seat. "Are you all right? Did you want to talk to Mrs. Barton, or—"

"I'm fine, Mrs. Clelland. Really." Miranda smiled. "This was helpful. I wasted too much energy last year worrying about Victor and his little buddies." She stared at Colby, who avoided her gaze. "But now I know I don't need anything from them. Because what they think doesn't matter at all."

Miranda walked out with her head held high.

Victor was turning a sickly shade of green, and Colby was maybe thinking about digging a tunnel through the floor. Honestly, I kind of enjoyed that.

"Do you want a break?" Mrs. Clelland asked Victor softly. He shook his head.

"It's OK." He turned to me. "Do you want to go, Brian? You probably have the longest list." He attempted a smile that quickly faded. I wasn't smiling back.

My heart raced. Ezra lightly touched my shoulder. My brain instantly called up a catalog of terrible things Victor had said to me. *Loser. Freak. Ghost. Do you talk at all anymore? I swear you're going psycho on us.*

"I don't want to give you a list. I'm not sure I want an apology either. I just want to know *why*." I met Victor's eyes. "Why me? What made you decide in the first week of seventh grade that you were going to torture me all year?"

Victor hesitated. "It's going to sound ridiculous," he finally admitted.

"I'm not expecting a *good* reason. But I still want to hear it."

"Yeah, I figured." He picked at his thumbnail. "I quit playing hockey right before seventh grade. My dad's obsessed with hockey. He tells this terrible joke: If the Pope and the Stanley Cup were falling off a bridge and he only had time to save one, at least the Pope would go to heaven."

He rolled his eyes. "My brothers are just as bad. They both think they'll make the NHL. And I was good too, except I hated it. So I quit. Mom stuck up for me, but that didn't help much. My brothers treated me like crap, and Dad kept lecturing me about not being a quitter. Then I sold all my gear online, and when he found out, he was so mad, he stopped talking to me."

Victor glanced at me. "You're wondering what this has to do with you, right? The day before school started, I went out on my scooter to get away from home for a while, and I saw you playing basketball at the park with your dad and your brother. You were all laughing, and I was kind of jealous. Then the next day, I said hi to you in homeroom, and you practically ran away from me."

I blinked. "Victor, I wasn't being snobby. It was my first day at a new school, and I have major social anxiety. I was overwhelmed."

"Yeah, I figured that out too. You were so quiet. It made it easier to pick on you." He rubbed his face. "I was just angry. I know that's no excuse . . ."

"Yeah, it's not." I looked Victor in the eye. "I don't have a perfect family, you know. My dad's in jail."

Victor's eyes widened. Someone else gasped, and a flash of anxiety coursed through me. The only people in the room who knew about my dad were my friends and Mrs. Clelland. I wasn't ashamed of him, but it also wasn't the kind of thing I wanted to broadcast in junior high. But I needed to say it to Victor.

"When I punched you, I was stressed out because my family was so messed up that I couldn't even stay at home. I ended up living with Mrs. Clelland for two weeks." More murmurs, but I focused on Victor. "Still, I felt bad about it, so I said sorry. Because having your own problems isn't an excuse to make other people miserable. It doesn't even fix anything. It just turns you into a jerk."

Dead silence. Mrs. Clelland was looking at me with misty-eyed concern. But I didn't feel panicky. Saying all that felt . . . good.

"I know that now." Victor sighed. "I guess I always knew it, deep down. And I'm sorry. I was definitely a jerk." He glanced at me and looked away. "And maybe I was jealous because you got better grades in everything but math. You're so smart, it's disgusting."

"You are really smart," Matt echoed.

"And you're super nice," Madi added.

"And an excellent baller, Spicy B," Ty chimed in.

Ezra nudged me with his elbow. "You can even beat Kevan in a hot wing eating contest."

"That contest was rigged!" Kevan protested. "But you are the coolest white guy I know, B. Once again, no offense to other white people in the room."

"You are a little bit cool." Victor gave me a tiny smile. "I wish I realized that earlier."

After being invisible for so long, it still felt weird when people complimented me, and it was even weirder coming from Victor.

I watched him as another kid went, and I thought of my favorite scene in *The Voyage of the Dawn Treader*. This rotten kid named Eustace Scrubb had turned into a dragon, and to become a boy again he had to peel off all his scales, layer by layer. It was painful, like ripping scabs from his whole body, but it felt good at the same time. When it was finally over, he was a changed kid—braver and kinder and not so selfish.

Watching Victor say *I'm sorry* over and over was like watching him shed layers of dragon skin.

Eventually he turned to Alicia. "Your turn."

Her eyes narrowed. "You bet it's my turn."

34. BOHEMIAN RHAPSODY, PART III

EZRA

"You used me." Alicia glared at Victor. "You made me think you liked me, then you just disappeared. No calls, no texts, nothing all summer. Like I didn't exist anymore." Her voice shook. "I spent *so long* trying to figure out what I did wrong. Then I realized it wasn't me. It was you. 'Cause you're the worst."

Mrs. Clelland leaned forward like she was about to correct Alicia for breaking the *no personal attacks* rule, but Victor spoke first.

"You're right. It wasn't you. You're pretty, and funny, and amazing. And I messed up."

He paused for a long time. I could tell he was still afraid to say more. The last half hour had been hard for him, and honestly, it had been tough to watch. Victor used to be *awful*. He had a supervillain's ability to uncover what would make people feel the worst about themselves, then he'd used it against them. It was ugly, and it made me wonder how I could have feelings for someone who'd act like that.

But the amazing thing was he had the opposite ability too. He noticed people's strengths. Every time he gave the perfect compliment to someone he used to torment, the air in the room grew lighter. And something was changing in him. I could see it.

"Victor," I said. "It's OK."

He met my eyes before he looked back at the floor and started talking.

"I had a hard summer. I was already feeling bad about stuff at school, and Ty's party, and then my parents split up."

Alicia drew in a breath. "Oh."

Victor shrugged. "I knew it was for the best. And I knew it wasn't really about me. Mom and Dad fought over everything, not just me and hockey. Mom and I spent the summer at my grandparents' place in New Brunswick, and I was glad to be away from Dad and my brothers. But once we got there, and I didn't have much to do, everything hit me." He glanced at Alicia. "I know I should have called or texted. I thought about it every day. But it was like I got stuck in quicksand. I spent a lot of time in bed."

"It sounds like you were depressed," Brian said.

Victor exhaled. "Maybe. Everything seemed pointless. Colby was the only person I kept in touch with. He joked around with me, and that helped."

Colby shook his head. "I didn't even know how bad it was, bro. Not until . . ."

"The alien abduction? That was everyone's favorite rumor, right?" Victor looked around. A few people giggled nervously.

His eyes settled on me again. "The truth is pretty embarrassing. I went walking in the woods behind my grandparents' place, and when I found a river, I went swimming. The current was stronger than I thought, and I drifted too far to swim back. The brush was so thick along the riverbank that I couldn't just follow the shore back, either. And I got caught in a thunderstorm. One minute it was sunny, then *bam*. So I tried to find shelter, and I got turned around." He shook his head. "I felt like such a clueless city noob."

"How long were you out there?" Ty asked.

"Most of the night." Victor squeezed his fists, like he was trying to keep himself under control. "They called in a search team and divers after my grandfather found my clothes by the river. Everyone assumed the worst."

Kevan sat up. "They found your clothes?"

"I went swimming, remember? And I was alone, so . . ." Victor exhaled. "Just so you know, spending the night in the woods in nothing but your underwear is the worst. It's cold, mosquitoes treat you like a walking taco, and even when you get rescued, you want to die of embarrassment. I give it zero stars."

Madi let out one shocked "Ha!" but every guy in the room cringed. That sounded awful. Being in your underwear onstage at a school assembly would be almost as bad, but it would be over quicker and it wouldn't be as scary, or itchy.

Matt gulped. "That must have been horrible."

"Yeah," Victor said. "I spent a day in the hospital. And my mom figured that disappearing in the woods was a cry for help or something, so she took me to a therapist when we got home. That turned out to be good, though. Dr. Wright's helped me a lot."

"Therapy's great, right?" Brian said. His face had changed too. The anger was gone.

"Yeah." Victor turned to Alicia. "I was too embarrassed to tell you any of that. And by the time I came back here in November, it was too late to make things right. I'm really sorry."

A tear slipped down Alicia's cheek. "Victor, *I'm* sorry. I had no idea what you were going through."

Victor shook his head. "I'll always be sorry I messed things up, but I hope we can be friends someday."

"Maybe." Alicia sighed. "You like some other girl now, don't you? That's who you were apologizing to in the announcements."

"Not exactly. I did this because I needed to do it." Victor swallowed hard. "But, uh, I actually fell for this amazing guy. He's funny, and talented, and really kind. He's just *himself*. He makes me want to be better. And I'm just sorry I hurt him." Victor's voice went shaky. "Um, your turn, Ezra."

I knew everyone was looking at me, and I didn't care. I was focused on Victor. His knee bounced as he clenched his hands together, and it made me think there was something he was still holding back. But maybe he wasn't ready to say it here, and that was OK.

"I'm not mad. I forgive you." I smiled at him. "I'm so glad you did this."

Relief flooded his face, and he smiled back. "Me too."

A silence fell over the room.

Mrs. Clelland looked around. "Wow. All of you—thank you. I'm so proud of you." She dabbed at her eye with a tissue. "We have a few minutes before the bell rings. Victor, do you want to say anything before I close us off?"

"Wait," Brian interrupted. "Before you do that, I'm sorry I yelled at you earlier, Victor. Ezra's been telling me that you're trying to change, and I didn't totally believe it. Maybe I didn't want to believe it, because it was easier to keep thinking of you as the villain. But that's not fair, and I'm sorry."

Victor blinked. For the first time, he looked lost, like he had no idea what to do with Brian's apology.

"Me too," Matt added. "When there were a bunch of rumors going around, I talked a lot of trash about you. Now that I know the whole story, I feel bad about it. Sorry."

Kevan scratched his head. "Yeah, same. The idea that you'd been sucked into the Upside Down was too good to resist. I'm sorry."

"I get it," Victor said. "No hard feelings."

"Victor, I . . ." Mrs. Clelland paused. "I owe you an apology too."

His eyes went wide.

"You're very smart, and I believe I've treated you fairly in the classroom. But I also noticed your attitude, and I've been teaching long enough that I wasn't optimistic you would change." Mrs. Clelland drew a shuddery breath. "I'm sorry for that, but I'm glad you've proven me wrong."

Victor was blinking hard.

Mrs. Clelland kept going. "You've come a long way this year. You've made mistakes, and you'll probably make more—because we all do—but you're *trying*. I've met your father, and I taught your brothers, and . . . well, I know how hard it is to break the cycle in a toxic environment. But what you did today was a difficult and beautiful thing. And I am so, so proud of you."

Mrs. Clelland was teary. Alicia and Madi were too. Heck, so was I.

Victor squeezed his fists and his face turned pink. "Thanks, Mrs. Clelland, and everyone, and . . . I have to go to the bathroom." With a panicked look, he raced for the door.

"Victor?" Mrs. Clelland called, but he kept going.

I hurried after him. He turned in the opposite direction of the bathroom, and I knew instantly where he was headed. I followed him into the band room. It was empty today, and Victor sat at the piano bench with his head in his hands.

"Ezra, I need a minute," he said in a strained voice.

I sat and put an arm around him. He tensed at first, but I didn't move, and his shoulders loosened. Slowly, he uncovered his face.

"That was really brave," I told him. "Are you OK?"

"I think so." He exhaled. "It was hard. But you were right. I needed to face it."

A few strands of hair had fallen into his face, and I brushed them back. He was blinking a lot and his breathing was ragged. My heart sped up. I touched his cheek. He swallowed.

"Are we going to, uh . . ."

"Yes," I said. And I kissed him.

It was way better than "Bohemian Rhapsody."

If I ever get to play a concert in an arena full of screaming fans, I hope it would feel as good as my first kiss with Victor.

He wrapped his arms around me, and I pulled him closer. "Oh!"

I opened my eyes. Mrs. Clelland was standing by the door, with Brian, Colby, Kevan, and Ty.

She cleared her throat. "I wanted to make sure Victor was OK."

"Looks like they're both OK," Kevan cracked, and Colby snorted. Victor and I let each other go. My cheeks were burning, but I tried to play it cool as I straightened my glasses.

"Yeah, we're good," I said, as casually as I could manage.

It sunk in that I'd just kissed a guy. In school. In front of my friends, and they were all grinning at me. Even Colby.

I took Victor's hand. And he burst into tears.

I didn't even think before I pulled him into a hug. He practically fell into me, like he could barely hold himself up. In a second, Brian crossed the room to join us. The others followed, and soon we were one big pile holding on to each other.

"So," I said. "We should probably talk about the woods."

Victor's nose wrinkled. "Do we have to? I've already had a month's worth of feelings today. Feelings are awful."

I knew he was joking, but I didn't let him off the hook. "If you're going to be my boyfriend, and the keyboard player in my band, this is part of the deal."

Victor tilted his head. "We're starting a band?"

"We'll talk about that later. This comes first."

He sighed. "Fine."

We were in my basement after school. Victor was sprawled on the couch next to me like he owned the place, even though it was only his third time in my house. It was cute enough that I was tempted to skip straight to kissing, but we needed to talk. Also, Brian and Colby were here, so skipping straight to kissing would be rude.

Having the four of us together felt a little awkward, but it was important. And it wasn't going as badly as I feared. After everything at lunch, Brian was more relaxed around Victor and Colby. He was lying on his belly on the floor, looking at his phone. Colby was quieter than usual, parked in a beanbag chair in the corner.

Victor bit into a carrot stick with a sharp *crack*. "So, what do you want to know about the worst night of my life?"

I had a dozen questions, but Brian glanced up and cut right to it.

"When you went into the woods, did you want to come out?"

Victor was quiet for long enough that my stomach sank.

"I'm not sure," he finally said.

I cleared my throat. "What does that mean?"

Victor sat up. "It means I felt so bad that I didn't care what happened anymore. I wasn't trying to get lost, but I wasn't trying not to, either."

I swallowed hard. "It makes me sad to think of you out there, hopeless and cold and alone."

"Me too," Colby said.

Huh. Colby admitting he has feelings is a new development.

"I get it, though." Brian propped up onto his elbows. "I had some bad nights too. But on my worst one, Ezra, Kevan, and Ty showed up in a snowstorm and helped me through it."

I remembered how useless I'd felt when I left Brian's house that night. But he'd talked to us, so I guess it had helped. And I'd talked to Mom that night. Now that I look back, that had helped me too. Something had changed between Mom and me.

Victor shifted to lie back, with his feet dangling over the end of the couch and his head resting on my lap. He took my hand and held it against his chest, with his hand on top of mine. He looked up, sort of sideways, and it was like he was letting me see him from a new angle. No hiding, no pretending. Just Victor.

"The thing is, once I realized I was lost, I didn't want to be lost anymore," he said.

Brian nodded. "You had to know you were a dragon before you could stop being a dragon."

Colby wrinkled his nose. "What does that even mean?"

"No, I get it," Victor said. "You're so smart, Brian."

"You don't have to be super nice to me forever," Brian replied. "Just for two more weeks, then I'll officially forgive you."

Victor laughed, and my hand bounced against his chest. "Deal."

"You know, you're kind of funny, now that you talk more," Colby said to Brian. He shot me a guilty look. "Ezra tried to tell me that a while ago. Sorry I messed up so bad."

"You don't have to apologize forever either," I told him. "You can have the same two-week deal."

"Oh. OK."

"I'm just messing with you, Colby. Hey, what happened to Jackson after that party?"

Colby grinned. "He's grounded for the rest of the school year. Mom and Dad lit him *up*. I've never seen them so mad. Usually they believe Jackson over me, but not this time. It helped that your mom got involved, Ezra." He tucked his hands behind his head. "It's nice not being the disappointing son for once."

As Colby told his story, in typical Colby style, for a second I wondered if we'd ever go back to how we used to be. But the thought passed, because I didn't really want that. I had good memories from when we were younger, but I realized now that I let Colby get away with things that weren't OK. I'd made myself smaller for the sake of our friendship, but real friends help you grow, not shrink.

Maybe we'd both grown enough that we could start over. But we didn't have to figure that out today. He was here now, and so was my best friend who helped me be brave enough to be myself, and so was the boy who liked me enough to place his warm beating heart in my hand. That was enough to make today a good day.

EPILOGUE: BIG MAN

BRIAN

"Rise and shine, Big Man. Gonna be a great day today."

Dad's voice jolted me from a dream. As I woke up, my anxious brain ramped into fourth gear.

Instant morning panic
If Dad's waking me,
then my alarm didn't go off,
which means I overslept,
which means I'm running late—

My face must have given away what my mind was doing. Dad ruffled my hair. "Breathe, kiddo. You're skipping school today, remember? Take your time. Breakfast will be ready in ten." He grinned. "Happy birthday, Brian."

After he left, I gathered my bearings. I was extra groggy because Dad and I had stayed up late watching the NBA Finals. Gabe, Ty, and Ezra texted with me through the game. Ty was a diehard LeBron James fan, and he was devastated when Golden State won again, taking a 3–0 series lead for the second year in a row. Gabe was thrilled.

I checked my phone. It was after eight, so my friends were at school, and they'd messaged me already.

Ezra: Salutations young whippersnapper

Ezra's birthday was four days ago, and our enormous age difference had been a running joke all week.

Ty: Happy Bday. Everything is trash but you're the one thing worth celebrating

Poor Ty. I guess he still wasn't over Cleveland's loss.

Kevan: Happy birthday bruh! Wait'll you see the cake I made for tonight. It's epic

My stomach rumbled thinking about Kevan's desserts. Or maybe because I smelled bacon.

Victor: happy birthday boogerjuice

I wrote him back. **Thanks donkey breath**
Exactly two weeks after we'd hung out in Ezra's basement, Victor had turned to me after school and said, *"Time's up. I don't have to be nice to you anymore, turdbucket."*

I'd laughed. Now we traded ridiculous insults every day. It was one of my favorite rituals. Three weeks ago, Ms. Floriman had heard Victor yell, *"What's up, you cosmic outhouse!"* and immediately called him into her office. I had to follow and explain that he wasn't bullying me, and I thought it was funny. She'd looked skeptical, until I threw my arm around him.

"I know it's hard to believe," I'd said, *"but I've grown fond of this sentient armpit fungus colony."*

Victor had cracked up. *"That's brilliant. I wish I'd thought of it."*

Ms. Floriman had stared at us like maybe we'd both been sniffing Sharpies. *"That's good news, but tone it down in the hall,"* she said before letting us go.

I couldn't blame her for being confused. If anyone told me a year ago that Victor and I would get along, I wouldn't have believed them.

As I put my phone down and hopped out of bed, a flutter of anxiety kicked in again. Today was June 7, my fourteenth birthday. One year after the worst day of my life.

Dad was home, unlike last year, so that helped. Still, the flutter didn't fade until I got dressed and reached the kitchen. Dad was frying bacon, and Mom was pouring hot water into the teapot.

She's up. She's fine. Nothing bad is going to happen.

I let out a slow breath. Mom heard. She came straight to me and wrapped her arms around me. I didn't have to explain the irrational thoughts bouncing around my head.

She knew. She didn't even say anything; she just held me, and I hugged her tight.

Dad slid three plates of bacon and buckwheat pancakes onto the table. "Breakfast is served."

We dug in. So far, fourteen wasn't so bad.

After I'd eaten, Dad took me shopping. He was working Saturday at his new construction job so he could take today off. I said I didn't want anything big for my birthday, but my basketball shoes were getting small and I needed a new pair for the summer.

I'd made the provincial team with Ty. It felt pretty darn good.

Dad cranked the stereo as we drove, and the bass rattled our chests. I was so glad to have him home, but it had been harder than I expected at first. After most of a year without him, we had to figure out how we fit together again. Dad was in the bathroom when I was trying to get ready for school. Dad was making Richie's lunch and ruining his ham sandwich. (For Richie, mayo was an unforgivable sin.) Dad was having whispered conversations with Mom that set me on edge, even if I couldn't hear the details.

Naturally, my garbage brain worried constantly. I worried about Richie, who sulked and slammed doors and spent more time at the Sidhus'. I worried that Dad looked exhausted after long shifts, and I worried that maybe he had to work so hard because money was tight. I worried that so much change would send Mom into a bad place.

With all that on my mind, I had a wicked panic attack in early May, two weeks after Dad came home. It hit me in school, just before lunch, and I staggered outside and curled against the wall. It was my first attack in months, and I was terrified it would send me back into the hole I'd been in over the winter. But Ezra found me and sat with me. It still sucked, but he took care of me. The next day was better. And now . . . well, we were all figuring it out together.

Dad took me to Courtside Sneakers, this indie shop with a killer selection. Having a wall full of options was hard on my indecisive brain, but we were the first customers of the morning, and the guy behind the counter was happy to pull a bunch of pairs for me to try.

"They have to be durable," Dad said. "He's on the provincial team. He'll be playing a lot of ball this summer."

"Oh yeah?" The salesman looked impressed.

"You should see him light it up from long range," Dad crowed. "He hit seven threes in his junior high championship game."

OK, that's a little much, Dad.

The guy whistled. "Well, let's take care of your feet then, so you can keep that hot hand."

Eventually I settled on Nikes a lot like the pair I'd bought last fall, only two sizes bigger. Dad shook his head as we left. "Size *eleven*. Slow down with all that growing, Big Man."

Dad used to call me B-Man, but Big Man was his go-to nickname now. I liked it.

He glanced at the car's clock. "We've got time for a game and showers before lunch. What do you think?"

"Sure," I said. "Don't know if I'll break a sweat beating you, though."

Dad howled. "You grew an ego too, huh? Don't run your mouth if you can't back it up."

The park was empty except for a daycare group on the playground when we pulled up to the court. I didn't want to wreck my new shoes playing outside, so I squeezed into my old ones. We shot for a few minutes to warm up, then we played a game of Twenty-one.

Dad used to let me win when I was little, then he took it easy enough that the games were close, then he won but he had to work for it. Today, though, my newly fourteen-year-old self was confident. Dad was way stronger than me, but I was quicker, and as tall as him now. And my jump shot was, let's be honest, a work of art.

He let me have first ball, and I immediately hit him with a crossover, step back *swish*. He shook his head.

I did break a sweat, because the game was rough. Dad bumped and jostled and knocked me on my butt once when he tried to drive past me for a layup. He winced, like maybe he'd pushed too far, but I hopped up quickly.

"Don't worry," I told him. "I can take it."

I ended up whupping him, 21–12.

"You're probably still rusty," I said on the way home. "I'm sure you'll do better next time."

Dad snorted. "You're so obnoxious now. I love it." He pinched my arm, and I squirmed away, laughing.

After we cleaned up, and I'd bragged about my victory to Mom, we swung by the elementary school to spring Richie early for lunch. He did a celebration shimmy as he burst through the front doors, a free fifth grader.

"Happy birthday!" he greeted me as he slid in the back seat. "I can't believe Mom and Dad let you skip *all day*." He leaned toward the front seat. "Since my birthday's in August, I should get a free skip day before school ends."

"Deal," Dad said.

We headed to the Hungry Chili, where I consumed a mountain of Hot Numbing Chicken. We'd had takeout pizza to celebrate when Dad was released, but between Mom's and Dad's conflicting work schedules and everything else, this was our first time in a restaurant since he'd been home.

It was all I wanted for my birthday—the four of us, together.

I took a nap when we got home, because even good things could feel overwhelming. And later in the afternoon, Dad drove me to Ty's house. Parties weren't my thing, but my friends had insisted on throwing a dual Brian-and-Ezra birthday bash.

Ezra was already there when I arrived, and he and Ty greeted me at the door.

"It's our boy!" Ezra exclaimed. "Look how much he's grown, Ty." He tried to pinch my cheek. I slapped his hand away.

"How'd band practice go?" I asked.

"Mostly good," Ezra said. "Caleb's still allergic to slow songs, but we're working on it."

"You pick a name yet?" Brittany called from somewhere behind him.

"Not yet," Ezra said. "My current favorite is Black Rainbow."

"Ooh, I like it!"

I accepted Ty's five-step handshake-to-shoulder bump greeting and stepped inside. The living room was crowded already. Ty's parents and Mrs. Clelland hovered behind Gabe and Brittany, who were dressed up like movie stars. They both pulled me into a hug.

"Happy birthday," Gabe said in my ear.

"I can't believe you came here on your prom night." I took in Gabe's blue suit and gold tie. "And I can't believe Brittany actually let you wear Golden State colors."

Brittany gestured to her own shimmering gold pantsuit. "We made a deal. He gets his Steph Curry cosplay, and I don't have to wear a dress."

"We need pictures!" Mrs. Clelland declared.

I looked down at my white T-shirt and basketball shorts. "Really?"

"Don't argue," Gabe whispered. "She's gone full Prom Mom. It's terrifying."

"I'm allowed to be sentimental on my son's prom night." Mrs. Clelland snapped her fingers. "Come on, all of you. Let's go."

"Yes ma'am!" Ty saluted. He called Kevan and Colby from the kitchen. Ty's mom suggested the backyard would be more scenic, and we were parading through the yard when Victor arrived.

He greeted us with a confused half smile. "Uh, what's happening?"

"Pictures. Come on." Ezra grabbed his hand, and Victor rolled with it.

Some things had changed in the last two and a half months, but change could be good. Ty and I hung out a lot now. We practiced every weekend with the provincial team, and sometimes we went out with the team afterward, or chilled here at his place. He still showed up before school to shoot with me too. Ezra didn't come as often. Victor usually got dropped off at his house and they walked to school together. They also spent lots of time rehearsing with their band or "recording" together. We'd all started saying "recording" with air quotes, because we were convinced they spent half their time kissing. Ezra seemed happier than ever.

Kevan and Colby were hanging out again too. Colby and I weren't close or anything, but he was friendly enough when we were all together. And Victor, well . . .

After we finished with photos and Gabe and Brittany headed off with Mrs. Clelland ("To take a thousand more pictures in the Public Gardens," Gabe said with a sigh), Victor untangled from Ezra and pressed a gift into my hands. "This is for you, toadpimple."

I could tell from the shape and weight that it was a book. There was an envelope attached with my name on it and the ugliest little stick figure drawing. The eyes were enormous and the ears were lopsided. It was hideous. I loved it.

"You got me a present?"

Victor scratched his head. "Don't look so shocked. It's your birthday, remember?"

"We all got you presents, Spicy B," Ty said.

I looked around at them, and I couldn't help but think that a year ago I didn't have any friends at all, and I was in a stranger's house, feeling lost and abandoned. I couldn't have dreamed that I'd be this happy today.

I swallowed hard. "This is my best birthday ever."

Victor raised his eyebrows. "Are you getting emotional?"

Ty laughed. "Have you met Brian? Of course he's getting emotional. Let's eat before he starts hugging everybody."

We ate burgers on the deck, and afterward Kevan brought out the cake. It had white frosting with *Happy Birthday Brian and Ezra* spelled out in dark orange icing. Two cookie decorations—one shaped like a guitar and one like a basketball—stuck out of the top.

"I know you don't like things too sweet, so it's cardamom carrot cake with cream cheese icing," Kevan said.

Colby's nose wrinkled. "That sounds weird."

"Don't eat any, then," Kevan shot back. "More for us."

Colby punched his shoulder. "Of course I'll eat it. You know I like your food. Even the weird stuff. As long as it's not too spicy."

"So basic," Kevan muttered.

"Quit bickering and light it up," Ty said.

Kevan lit the candles, there was some loud and dramatic singing, and Ezra and I blew out the candles together.

"I think we got exactly seven each," Ezra said. "Did you make a wish?"

I shrugged. "I didn't need to."

Kevan cut us each a slice and urged me to take the first bite.

I sighed happily. "This is perfect, Kev. It's exactly the right amount of sweet, and the cinnamon and cardamom give it a nice zing."

Ezra held his slice of the orange cake beside my face. "And it's a perfect match for Brian's hair."

Kevan grinned. "I'll call it the Spicy B Special."

"OK, bro, let us at it already," Colby said.

Kevan cut pieces for Ty's parents, then it was a frenzy. In two minutes, there was nothing left but crumbs.

"Kev, you remain a culinary genius," Ty said happily. "Now, we jump in the pool."

Kevan stared at Ty's above-ground pool. "It's only the beginning of June. Today's the first warm day all week. The water's probably freezing."

"Yeah, it's cold," Ty agreed. "But we have to jump. It's tradition."

"What tradition?"

"The tradition of Brian and Ezra's Annual Birthday Jam."

"Annual? This is the first one!"

"Exactly. We have to establish protocol."

"But—"

"Let's do it," Victor interrupted. He pulled off his shirt, and Ezra whistled at him.

Colby laughed. "Why are you like this?"

"I like what I like," Ezra said, grinning. "Are you coming?"

"Of course." Colby took off his tank top.

Ezra turned to me. "Brian?"

"You bet."

Soon we were standing with our toes curled at the edge of the deck, overlooking the pool.

"Mom, take a picture with my phone," Ty called over his shoulder.

"You boys and your foolishness," she mumbled, but she slid into place. "All right, I'm ready."

"Wait!" Ezra said. "We have to jump together." He held my hand. "On three. Brian, you count it."

I reached for Ty's hand on my other side. "One!" I yelled. "Two! Three!"

And we jumped.

AUTHOR'S NOTE

My local basketball community has meant a lot to me for a long time. Unfortunately, we've lost some wonderful people far too early.

I believe things are moving in the right direction when it comes to mental health in sports. I'm grateful for pros like DeMar DeRozan and Kevin Love, who have helped open the door for more honest conversations, especially among boys and men. But there's still further to go.

If you're struggling or know someone who's struggling, please reach out for help. We all need help sometimes. Talk to a trusted adult or call a support line where trained professionals are waiting to talk to you.

In the United States, you can call the 988 Suicide and Crisis Lifeline or find resources at 988lifeline.org/help-yourself/youth.

In Canada, you can call the Kids Help Phone at 1-800-668-6868, text CONNECT to 686868, or find resources online at kidshelpphone.ca.

ACKNOWLEDGMENTS

Bringing a book into the world is a team effort, and I'm grateful I get to work with the great team at Abrams Kids. Thanks to my editor, Emily Daluga, who loves and understands these characters so well that most of her editorial suggestions made me go, *Wow, I should have thought of that.* Thanks as well to Megan Carlson, Chelsea Hunter, Rachael Marks, the marketing and publicity team, and artist Nick Blanchard for capturing the spirit of this book again on the cover.

I'm also thrilled to be part of the team at McIntosh & Otis. Thanks again to Christa Heschke and Daniele Hunter for being such great sounding boards and champions of my work.

My gratitude as always to Team Lucas, for putting up with my disappearing into fictional worlds and rooting for me every step of the way.

Friends and colleagues make the writing journey easier, and I'm thankful for my Slacker crew and friends at Middle Grade Authorcade. My appreciation to Eric Bell and Mary E. Roach for their thoughtful feedback on early drafts of this book, and a special thanks to Dr. Lyssa Mia Smith for her professional insights into working with teenagers facing mental health challenges.

Thank you to everyone in the middle grade community who enthusiastically supported *Thanks A Lot, Universe*, every teacher and librarian who helped it reach their students, and most of all to you—the readers. I'm grateful to everyone who has reached out to tell me how much my books have meant to them. I'm so glad I had a chance to tell more of Brian and Ezra's story, and I couldn't have done it without your support. Thank you!